FAIRY TALES

BY
THE
BROTHERS
GRIMM

FAIRY TALES

BY THE BROTHERS GRIMM
Illustrations by Allen Atkinson

WANDERER BOOKS
PUBLISHED BY SIMON & SCHUSTER, NEW YORK

llustrations copyright © 1982 by Allen Atkinson. All rights reserved including the right of reproduction in whole or in part in any form. Published by WANDERER BOOKS, a Simon & Schuster Division of Gulf & Western Corporation, Simon & Schuster Building, 1230 Avenue of the Americas, New York, New York 10020

Designed by Jonette Jakobson-Kragic Manufactured in the United States of America 10 9 8 7 6 5 4 3 2 1

WANDERER and colophon are trademarks of Simon & Schuster

Also available in Julian Messner Certified Edition

Library of Congress Cataloging in Publication Data Main entry under title: Fairy tales. Translation of: Kinder- und Hausmärchen.
  "A Wanderer book."
  Summary: A collection of fairy tales collected in Germany by two brothers.
  1. Fairy tales—Germany. [1. Fairy tales. 2. Folklore— German] I. Grimm, Jacob, 1785–1863. II. Grimm, Wilhelm, 1786–1859. III. Atkinson, Allen, ill. PZ8.F168597 398.2'1'0943 81-16646 ISBN 0-671-43792-5 AACR2

CONTENTS

long time ago there lived a king whose wisdom was noised abroad in all the country. Nothing remained long unknown to him, and it was as if the knowledge of hidden things was brought to him in the air. However, he had one curious custom. Every day at dinner, after the table had been cleared and every one gone away, a trusty servant had to bring in one other dish. But it was covered up, and the servant himself did not know what was in it, and no one else knew, for the king waited until he was quite alone before he uncovered it. This had gone on a long time, but at last there came a day when the servant could restrain his curiosity no longer, but as he was carrying the dish away he took it into his own room. As soon as he had fastened the door securely, he lifted the cover, and there he saw a white snake lying on the dish. After seeing it he could not resist the desire to taste it, and so he cut off a small piece and put it in his mouth. As soon as it touched his tongue he heard outside his window a strange chorus of delicate voices. He went and listened, and

found that it was the sparrows talking together, and telling each other all they had seen in the fields and woods. The virtue of the snake had given him power to understand the speech of animals.

Now it happened one day that the queen lost her most splendid ring, and suspicion fell upon the trusty servant, who had the general superintendence, and he was accused of stealing it. The king summoned him to his presence, and after many reproaches told him that if by the next day he was not able to name the thief he should be considered guilty, and punished. It was in vain that he protested his innocence; he could get no better sentence. In his uneasiness and anxiety he went out into the courtyard, and began to consider what he could do in so great a necessity. There sat the ducks by the running water and rested themselves, and plumed themselves with their flat bills, and held a comfortable chat. The servant stayed where he was and listened to them. They told how they had waddled about all yesterday morning and found good food; and then one of them said pitifully, "Something lies very heavy in my craw,—it is the ring that was lying under the queen's window; I swallowed it down in too great a hurry."

Then the servant seized her by the neck, took her into the kitchen, and said to the cook, "Kill this one, she is quite ready for cooking."

"Yes," said the cook, weighing it in her hand; "there will be no trouble of fattening this one—it has been ready ever so long."

She then slit up its neck, and when it was opened the queen's ring was found in its craw. The servant could now clearly prove his innocence, and in order to make up for the injustice he had suffered the king permitted him to ask some favor for himself, and also promised him the place of greatest honor in the royal household.

But the servant refused it, and only asked for a horse and money for travelling, for he had a fancy to see the world, and look about him a little. So his request was granted, and he set out on his way; and one day he came to a pool of water, by which he saw three fishes who had got entangled in the rushes, and were panting for water. Although fishes are usually considered dumb creatures, he understood very well their lament that they were to perish so miserably; and as he had a compassionate heart he dismounted from his horse, and put the three fishes back again into the water. They quivered all over with joy, stretched out their heads, and called out to him, "We will remember and reward thee, because thou hast delivered us." He rode on, and after a while he heard a small voice come up from the sand underneath his horse's feet. He listened, and understood how an ant-king was complaining, "If only these men would keep off, with their great awkward beasts! here comes this stupid horse treading

down my people with his hard hoofs!"

The man then turned his horse to the side-path, and the ant-king called out to him, "We will remember and reward thee!"

The path led him through a wood, and there he saw a father-raven and mother-raven standing by their nest and throwing their young ones out.

"Off with you! young gallows-birds!" cried they; "we cannot stuff you any more; you are big enough to fend for yourselves!" The poor young ravens lay on the ground, fluttering, and beating the air with their pinions, and crying, "We are poor helpless things, we cannot fend for ourselves, we cannot even fly! we can only die of hunger!"

Then the kind young man dismounted, killed his horse with his dagger, and left it to the young ravens for food. They came hopping up, feasted away at it, and cried, "We will remember and reward thee!"

So now he had to use his own legs, and when he had gone a long way he came to a great town. There was much noise and thronging in the streets, and there came a man on a horse, who proclaimed, "That the king's daughter seeks a husband, but he who wishes to marry her must perform a difficult task, and if he cannot carry it through successfully, he must lose his life."

Many had already tried, but had lost their lives, in vain. The young man, when he saw the king's daughter, was so dazzled by her great beauty, that he forgot all danger, went to the king and offered himself as a wooer.

Then he was led to the sea-side, and a gold ring was thrown into the water before his eyes. Then the king told him that he must fetch the ring up again from the bottom of the sea, saying, "If you come back without it, you shall be put under the waves again and again until you are drowned."

Every one pitied the handsome young man, but they went, and left him alone by the sea. As he was standing on the shore and thinking of what he should do, there came three fishes swimming by, none other than those he had set free. The middle one had a mussel in his mouth, and he laid it on the strand at the young man's feet; and when he took it up and opened it there was the gold ring inside! Full of joy he carried it to the king, and expected the promised reward;

but the king's daughter, proud of her high birth, despised him, and set him another task to perform. She went out into the garden, and strewed about over the grass ten sacks full of millet seed.

"By the time the sun rises in the morning you must have picked up all these," she said, "and not a grain must be wanting."

The young man sat down in the garden and considered how it was possible to do this task, but he could contrive nothing, and stayed there, feeling very sorrowful, and expecting to be led to death at break of day. But when the first beams of the sun fell on the garden he saw that the ten sacks were all filled, standing one by the other, and not even a grain was missing. The ant-king had arrived in the night with his thousands of ants, and the grateful creatures had picked up all the millet seed, and filled the sacks with great industry. The king's daughter came herself into the garden and saw with astonishment that the young man had performed all that had been given him to do. But she could not let her proud heart melt, but said, "Although he has completed the two tasks, he shall not be my bridegroom unless he brings me an apple from the tree of life."

The young man did not know where the tree of life was to be found, but he set out and went on and on, as long as his legs could carry him, but he had no hope of finding it.

When he had gone through three kingdoms he came one evening to a wood, and seated himself under a tree to go to sleep; but he heard a rustling in the boughs, and a golden apple fell into his hand. Immediately three ravens flew towards him, perched on his knee, and said,

"We are the three young ravens that you delivered from starving; when we grew big, and heard that you were seeking the golden apple, we flew over the sea to the end of the earth, where the tree of life stands, and we fetched the apple."

Full of joy the young man set off on his way home, and brought the golden apple to the king's beautiful daughter, who was without any further excuse.

So they divided the apple of life, and ate it together; and their hearts were filled with love, and they lived in undisturbed happiness to a great age.

here was once a girl who was lazy and would not spin, and her mother could not persuade her to it, do what she would. At last the mother became angry and out of patience, and gave her a good beating, so that she cried out loudly. At that moment the queen was going by; as she heard the crying, she stopped; and, going into the house, she asked the mother why she was beating her daughter, so that every one outside in the street could hear her cries.

The woman was ashamed to tell of her daughter's laziness, so she said, "I cannot stop her from spinning; she is for ever at it, and I am poor and cannot furnish her with flax enough."

Then the queen answered, "I like nothing better than the sound of the spinning-wheel, and always feel happy when I hear its humming; let me take your daughter with me to the castle—I have plenty of flax, she shall spin there to her heart's content."

The mother was only too glad of the offer, and the queen took the girl with her. When they reached the castle the queen showed her three rooms which were filled with the finest flax as full as they could hold.

"Now you can spin me this flax," said she, "and when you can show it me all done you shall have my eldest son for bridegroom; you may be poor, but I make nothing of that—your industry is dowry enough."

The girl was inwardly terrified, for she could not have spun the flax, even if she were to live to be a hundred years old, and were to sit spinning every day of her life from morning to evening. And when she found herself alone she began to weep, and sat so for three days without putting her hand to it. On the third day the queen came, and when she saw that nothing had been done of the spinning she was much surprised; but the girl excused herself by saying that she had not been able to begin because of the distress she was in at leaving her home and her mother. The excuse contented the queen, who said, however, as she went away, "To-morrow you must begin to work."

When the girl found herself alone again she could not tell how to help herself or what to do, and in her perplexity she went and gazed out of the window. There she saw three women passing by, and the first of them had a broad flat foot, the second had a big under-lip that hung down over her chin, and the third had a remarkably broad thumb. They all of them stopped in front of the window, and called out to know what it was that the girl wanted. She told them all her need, and they promised her their help, and said, "Then will you invite us to your wedding, and not be ashamed of us, and call us your cousins, and let us sit at your table; if you will promise this, we will finish off your flax-spinning in a very short time."

"With all my heart," answered the girl; "only come in now, and begin at once."

Then these same women came in, and she cleared a space in the first room for them to sit and carry on their spinning. The first one drew out the thread and moved the treddle that turned the wheel, the second moistened the thread, the third twisted it, and rapped with her finger on the table, and as often as she rapped a heap of yarn fell to the ground, and it was most beautifully spun. But the girl hid the three spinsters out of the queen's sight, and only showed her, as often as she came, the heaps of well-spun yarn; and there was no end to the praises she received. When the first room was empty they went on to the second, and then to the third, so that at last all was finished. Then the three women took their leave, saying to the girl, "Do not forget what you have promised, and it will be all the better for you."

So when the girl took the queen and showed her the empty rooms, and the great heaps of yarn, the wedding was at once arranged, and the bridegroom rejoiced that he should have so clever and diligent a

wife, and praised her exceedingly.

"I have three cousins," said the girl, "and as they have shown me a great deal of kindness, I would not wish to forget them in my good fortune; may I be allowed to invite them to the wedding, and to ask them to sit at table with us?"

The queen and the bridegroom said at once, "There is no reason against it."

So when the feast began in came the three spinsters in strange guise, and the bride said, "Dear cousins, you are welcome."

"Oh," said the bridegroom, "how come

you to have such dreadfully ugly relations?"

And then he went up to the first spinster and said, "How is it that you have such a broad flat foot?"

"With treading," answered she, "with treading."

Then he went up to the second and said, "How is it that you have such a great hanging lip?"

"With licking," answered she, "with licking."

Then he asked the third, "How is it that you have such a broad thumb?"

"With twisting thread," answered she, "with twisting thread."

Then the bridegroom said that from that time forward his beautiful bride should never touch a spinning-wheel.

And so she escaped that tiresome flax-spinning.

A certain man, who had lost almost all his money, resolved to set off with the little that was left him, and travel into the wide world. Then the first place he came to was a village, where the young people were running about crying and shouting. "What is the matter?" asked he. "See here," answered they, "we have got a mouse that we make dance to please us. Do look at him: what a droll sight it is! how he jumps about!" But the man pitied the poor little thing, and said, "Let the mouse go, and I will give you money." So he gave them some, and took the mouse and let him run; and he soon jumped into a hole that was close by, and was out of their reach.

Then he travelled on and came to another village, and there the children had got an ass that they made stand on its hind legs and tumble, at which they laughed and shouted, and gave the poor beast no rest. So the good man gave them also some money to let the poor ass alone.

At the next village he came to, the young people had got a bear that had been taught to dance, and they were plaguing the poor thing sadly. Then he gave them too some money to let the beast go, and the bear was very glad to get on his four feet, and seemed quite happy.

But the man had now given away all the money he had in the world, and had not a shilling in his pocket. Then said he to himself, "The king has heaps of gold in his treasury that he never uses; I cannot die of hunger, I hope I shall be forgiven if I borrow a little, and when I get rich again I will repay it all."

Then he managed to get into the treasury, and took a very little money; but as he came out the king's guards saw him; so they said he was a thief, and took him to the judge, and he was sentenced to be thrown into the water in a box. The lid of the box was full of holes to let in air, and a jug of water and a loaf of bread were given him.

Whilst he was swimming along in the water very sorrowfully, he heard something nibbling and biting at the lock; and all of a sudden it fell off, the lid flew open, and there stood his old friend the little mouse, who had done him this service. And then came the ass and the bear, and pulled the box ashore; and all helped him because he had been kind to them.

But now they did not know what to do next, and began to consult together; when on a sudden a wave threw on the shore a beautiful white stone that looked like an egg.

Then the bear said, "That's a lucky thing: this is the wonderful stone, and whoever has it may have every thing else that he wishes." So the man went and picked up the stone, and wished for a palace and a garden, and a stud of horses; and his wish was fulfilled as soon as he had made it. And there he lived in his castle and garden, with fine stables and horses; and all was so grand and beautiful, that he never could wonder and gaze at it enough.

After some time, some merchants passed by that way. "See," said they, "what a princely palace! The last time we were here, it was nothing but a desert waste." They were very curious to know how all this had happened; so they went in and asked the master of the palace how it had been so quickly raised. "I have done nothing myself," answered he, "it is the wonderful stone that did all."—"What a strange stone that must be!" said they: then he invited them in and showed it to them. They asked him whether he would sell it, and offered him all their goods for it; and the goods seemed so fine and costly, that he quite forgot that the stone would bring him in a moment a thousand better and richer things, and he agreed to make the bargain.

Scarcely was the stone, however, out of his hands before all his riches were gone, and he found himself sitting in his box in the water, with his jug of water and loaf of bread by his side. The grateful beasts, the mouse, the ass, and the bear, came directly to help him; but the mouse found she could not nibble off the lock this time, for it was a great deal stronger than before. Then the bear said, "We must find the wonderful stone again, or all our endeavours will be fruitless."

The merchants, meantime, had taken up their abode in the palace; so away went the three friends, and when they came near, the bear said, "Mouse, go in and look through the key-hole and see where the stone is kept: you are small, nobody will see you." The mouse did as she was told, but soon came back and said, "Bad news! I have looked in, and the stone hangs under the looking-glass by a red silk string, and on each side of it sits a great cat with fiery eyes to watch it."

Then the others took council together and said, "Go back again, and wait till the master of the palace is in bed asleep, then nip his nose and pull his hair." Away went the mouse, and did as they directed her; and the master jumped up very angry, and rubbed his nose, and cried, "Those rascally cats are good for nothing at all, they let the mice eat my very nose and pull the hair off my head." Then he hunted them out of the room; and so the mouse had the best of the game.

Next night as soon as the master was asleep, the mouse crept in again, and nibbled at the red silk string to which the stone hung, till down it dropped, and she rolled it along to the door; but when it got there, the poor

little mouse was quite tired; so she said to
the ass, "Put in your foot, and lift it over the
threshold." This was soon done: and they
took up the stone, and set off for the water
side. Then the ass said, "How shall we reach
the box?" But the bear answered, "That is
easily managed; I can swim very well, and do
you, donkey, put your fore feet over my

shoulder;—mind and hold fast, and take the stone in your mouth: as for you, mouse, you can sit in my ear."

It was all settled thus, and away they swam. After a time, the bear began to brag and boast: "We are brave fellows, are not we, ass?" said he; "what do you think?" But the ass held his tongue, and said not a word. "Why don't you answer me?" said the bear, "you must be an ill-mannered brute not to speak when you're spoken to." When the ass heard this, he could hold no longer; so he opened his mouth and dropped the wonderful stone. "I could not speak," said he; "did not you know I had the stone in my mouth? now 'tis lost, and that's your fault." "Do but hold your tongue and be quiet," said the bear; "and let us think what's to be done."

Then a council was held: and at last they called together all the frogs, their wives and families, relations and friends, and said: "A great enemy is coming to eat you all up; but never mind, bring us up plenty of stones, and we'll build a strong wall to guard you." The frogs hearing this were dreadfully frightened, and set to work, bringing up all the stones they could find. At last came a large fat frog pulling along the wonderful stone by the silken string: and when the bear saw it, he jumped for joy, and said, "Now we have found what we wanted." So he released the old frog from his load, and told him to tell his friends they might go about their business as soon as they pleased.

Then the three friends swam off again for the box; and the lid flew open, and they found that they were but just in time, for the bread was all eaten, and the jug almost empty. But as soon as the good man had the stone in his hand, he wished himself safe and sound in his palace again; and in a moment there he was, with his garden and his stables and his horses; and his three faithful friends dwelt with him, and they all spent their time happily and merrily as long as they lived.

here was once a wonderful musician, and he was one day walking through a wood all alone, thinking of this and that: and when he had nothing more left to think about, he said to himself, "I shall grow tired of being in this wood, so I will bring out a good companion."

So he took the fiddle that hung at his back and fiddled so that the wood echoed. Before long a wolf came through the thicket and trotted up to him.

"Oh, here comes a wolf! I had no particular wish for such company," said the musician: but the wolf drew nearer, and said to him, "Ho, you musician, how finely you play! I must learn how to play too."

"That is easily done," answered the musician, "you have only to do exactly as I tell you."

"O musician," said the wolf, "I will obey you, as a scholar does his master."

The musician told him to come with him. As they went a part of the way together they came to an old oak tree, which was hollow within and cleft through the middle.

"Look here," said the musician, "if you want to learn how to fiddle, you must put your fore feet in this cleft."

The wolf obeyed, but the musician took up a stone and quickly wedged both his paws with one stroke, so fast, that the wolf was a prisoner, and there obliged to stop.

"Stay there until I come back again," said the musician, and went his way.

After a while he said again to himself, "I shall grow weary here in this wood; I will bring out another companion," and he took his fiddle and fiddled away in the wood. Before long a fox came slinking through the trees.

"Oh, here comes a fox!" said the musician; "I had no particular wish for such company."

The fox came up to him and said, "O my dear musician, how finely you play! I must learn how to play too."

"That is easily done," said the musician, "you have only to do exactly as I tell you."

"O musician," answered the fox, "I will obey you, as a scholar his master."

"Follow me," said the musician; and as they went a part of the way together they came to a footpath with a high hedge on each side. Then the musician stopped, and taking hold of a hazel-branch bent it down to the earth, and put his foot on the end of it; then he bent down a branch from the other side, and said: "Come on, little fox, if you wish to learn something, reach me your left fore foot."

The fox obeyed, and the musician bound the foot to the left hand branch.

"Now, little fox," said he, "reach me the right one;" then he bound it to the right hand branch. And when he had seen that the knots were fast enough he let go, and the branches flew back and caught up the fox, shaking and struggling, in the air.

"Wait there until I come back again," said the musician, and went his way.

By and by he said to himself: "I shall grow weary in this wood; I will bring out another companion."

So he took his fiddle, and the sound

echoed through the wood. Then a hare sprang out before him.

"Oh, here comes a hare!" said he, "that's not what I want."

"Ah, my dear musician," said the hare, "how finely you play! I should like to learn how to play too."

"That is soon done," said the musician, "only you must do whatever I tell you."

"O musician," answered the hare, "I will obey you, as a scholar his master."

So they went a part of the way together, until they came to a clear place in the wood where there stood an aspen tree. The musician tied a long string round the neck of the hare, and knotted the other end of it to the tree.

"Now then, courage, little hare! run twenty times round the tree!" cried the musician, and the hare obeyed: as he ran round the twentieth time the string had wound twenty times round the tree trunk and the hare was imprisoned, and pull and tug as he would he only cut his tender neck with the string. "Wait there until I come back again," said the musician, and walked on.

The wolf meanwhile had struggled, and pulled, and bitten, at the stone, and worked away so long, that at last he made his paws free and got himself out of the cleft. Full of anger and fury he hastened after the musician to tear him to pieces. When the fox saw him run by he began groaning, and cried out with all his might, "Brother wolf, come and help me! the musician has betrayed me." The wolf then pulled the branches down, bit the knots in two, and set the fox free, and he went with him to take vengeance on the musician. They found the imprisoned hare, and set him likewise free, and then they all went on together to seek their enemy.

The musician had once more played his fiddle, and this time he had been more fortunate. The sound had reached the ears of a poor woodcutter, who immediately, and in spite of himself, left his work, and, with his axe under his arm, came to listen to the music.

"At last here comes the right sort of companion," said the musician; "it was a man I wanted, and not wild animals." And then he began to play so sweetly that the poor man stood as if enchanted, and his heart was filled with joy. And as he was standing there up came the wolf, the fox, and the hare, and he could easily see that they meant mischief. Then he raised his shining axe, and stood in front of the musician, as if to say, "Whoever means harm to him had better take care of himself, for he will have to do with me!"

Then the animals were frightened, and ran back into the wood, and the musician, when he had played once more to the man to show his gratitude, went on his way.

here was once a shoemaker, who, through no fault of his own, became so poor that at last he had nothing left but just enough leather to make one pair of shoes. He cut out the shoes at night, so as to set to work upon them next morning; and as he had a good conscience, he laid himself quietly down in his bed, committed himself to heaven, and fell asleep. In the morning, after he had said his prayers, and was going to get to work, he found the pair of shoes made and finished, and standing on his table. He was very much astonished, and could not tell what to think, and he took the shoes in his hand to examine them more nearly; and they were so well made that every stitch was in its right place, just as if they had come from the hand of a master-workman.

Soon after a purchaser entered, and as the shoes fitted him very well, he gave more than the usual price for them, so that the shoemaker had enough money to buy leather for two more pairs of shoes. He cut them out at night, and intended to set to work the next morning with fresh spirit; but that was not to be, for when he got up they were already finished, and a customer even was not lacking, who gave him so much money that he was able to buy leather enough for four new pairs. Early next morning he found the four pairs also finished, and so it always happened; whatever he cut out in the evening was worked up by the morning, so that he was soon in the way of making a good living, and in the end became very well to do.

One night, not long before Christmas, when the shoemaker had finished cutting out, and before he went to bed, he said to his wife, "How would it be if we were to sit up tonight and see who it is that does us this service?"

His wife agreed, and set a light to burn. Then they both hid in a corner of the room, behind some coats that were hanging up, and then they began to watch. As soon as it was midnight they saw come in two neatly-formed naked little men, who seated themselves before the shoemaker's table, and took up the work that was already prepared, and began to stitch, to pierce, and to hammer so cleverly and quickly with their little fingers that the shoemaker's eyes could scarcely follow them, so full of wonder was he. And they never left off until everything was finished and was standing ready on the table, and then they jumped up and ran off.

The next morning the shoemaker's wife

said to her husband, "Those little men have made us rich, and we ought to show ourselves grateful. With all their running about, and having nothing to cover them, they must be very cold. I'll tell you what; I will make little shirts, coats, waistcoats, and breeches for them, and knit each one of them a pair of stockings, and you shall make each of them a pair of shoes."

The husband consented willingly, and at night, when everything was finished, they laid the gifts together on the table, instead of the cut-out work, and placed themselves so

that they could observe how the little men would behave. When midnight came, they rushed in, ready to set to work, but when they found, instead of pieces of prepared leather, the neat little garments put ready for them, they stood a moment in surprise, and then they testified the greatest delight. With the greatest swiftness they took up the pretty garments and slipped them on, singing,

"What spruce and dandy boys are we!
No longer cobblers we will be."

Then they hopped and danced about, jumping over the chairs and tables, and at last they danced out at the door.

From that time they were never seen again; but it always went well with the shoemaker as long as he lived, and whatever he took in hand prospered.

(II)

There was once a poor servant maid, who was very cleanly and industrious; she swept down the house every day, and put the sweepings on a great heap by the door. One morning, before she began her work, she found a letter, and as she could not read, she laid her broom in the corner, and took the letter to her master and mistress, to see what it was about; and it was an invitation from the elves, who wished the maid to come and stand godmother to one of their children. The maid did not know what to do; and as she was told that no one ought to refuse the elves anything, she made up her mind to go. So there came three little elves, who conducted her into the middle of a high mountain, where the little people lived. Here everything was of a very small size, but more fine and elegant than can be told. The mother of the child lay in a bed made of ebony, studded with pearls, the counterpane was embroidered with gold, the cradle was of ivory, and the bathing-tub of gold. So the maid stood godmother, and was then for going home, but the elves begged her to stay at least three more days with them; and so she consented, and spent the time in mirth and jollity, and the elves seemed very fond of her. At last, when she was ready to go away, they filled her pockets full of gold, and led her back again out of the mountain. When she got back to the house, she was going to begin working again, and took her broom in her hand; it was still standing in the corner where she had left it, and began to sweep. Then came up some strangers and asked her who she was, and what she was doing. And she found that instead of three days, she had been seven years with the elves in the mountain, and that during that time her master and mistress had died. ⎯⎯⎯⎯⎯⎯

(III)

The elves once took a child away
from its mother, and left in its
place a changeling with a big
head and staring eyes, who did nothing but
eat and drink. The mother in her trouble
went to her neighbors and asked their advice. The neighbors told her to take the
changeling into the kitchen and put it near
the hearth, and then to make up the fire, and
boil water in two egg-shells; that would
make the changeling laugh, and if he
laughed, it would be all over with him. So
the woman did as her neighbors advised.
And when she set the egg-shells of water on
the fire, the changeling said,

"Though old I be
As forest tree,
Cooking in an egg-shell never did I see!"

and began to laugh. And directly there came
in a crowd of elves bringing in the right
child; and they laid it near the hearth, and
carried the changeling away with them.

n times past there lived a king and queen, who said to each other every day of their lives, "Would that we had a child!" and yet they had none. But it happened once that when the queen was bathing, there came a frog out of the water, and he squatted on the ground, and said to her, "Thy wish shall be fulfilled; before a year has gone by, thou shalt bring a daughter into the world."

And as the frog foretold, so it happened; and the queen bore a daughter so beautiful that the king could not contain himself for joy, and he ordained a great feast. Not only did he bid to it his relations, friends, and acquaintances, but also the wise women, that they might be kind and favorable to the child. There were thirteen of them in his kingdom, but as he had only provided twelve golden plates for them to eat from, one of them had to be left out. However, the feast was celebrated with all splendor; and as it drew to an end, the wise women stood forward to present to the child their wonderful gifts: one bestowed virtue, one beauty, a third riches, and so on, whatever there is in

the world to wish for. And when eleven of
them had said their say, in came the unin-
vited thirteenth, burning to revenge herself,
and without greeting or respect, she cried
with a loud voice, "In the fifteenth year of
her age the princess shall prick herself with a
spindle and shall fall down dead."

And without speaking one more word she
turned away and left the hall. Everyone was

terrified at her saying, when the twelfth came forward, for she had not yet bestowed her gift, and though she could not do away with the evil prophecy, yet she could soften it, so she said, "The princess shall not die, but fall into a deep sleep for a hundred years."

Now the king, being desirous of saving his child even from this misfortune, gave commandment that all the spindles in his kingdom should be burnt up.

The maiden grew up, adorned with all the gifts of the wise women; and she was so lovely, modest, sweet, and kind and clever, that no one who saw her could help loving her.

It happened one day, she being already fifteen years old, that the king and queen rode abroad, and the maiden was left behind alone in the castle. She wandered about into all the nooks and corners, and into all the chambers and parlors, as the fancy took her, till at last she came to an old tower. She climbed the narrow winding stair which led to a little door, with a rusty key sticking out of the lock; she turned the key, and the door opened, and there in the little room sat an old woman with a spindle, diligently spinning her flax.

"Good day, mother," said the princess, "what are you doing?"

"I am spinning," answered the old woman, nodding her head.

"What thing is that that twists round so briskly?" asked the maiden, and taking the spindle into her hand she began to spin; but no sooner had she touched it than the evil prophecy was fulfilled, and she pricked her finger with it. In that very moment she fell back upon the bed that stood there, and lay in a deep sleep. And this sleep fell upon the whole castle; the king and queen, who had returned and were in the great hall, fell fast asleep, and with them the whole court. The horses in their stalls, the dogs in the yard, the pigeons on the roof, the flies on the wall, the very fire that flickered on the hearth, became still, and slept like the rest; and the meat on the spit ceased roasting, and the cook, who was going to pull the scullion's hair for some mistake he had made, let him go, and went to sleep. And the wind ceased, and not a leaf fell from the trees about the castle.

Then round about that place there grew a hedge of thorns thicker every year, until at last the whole castle was hidden from view, and nothing of it could be seen but the vane on the roof. And a rumor went abroad in all the country of the beautiful sleeping Rosamond, for so was the princess called; and from time to time many kings' sons came and tried to force their way through the hedge; but it was impossible for them to do so, for the thorns held fast together like strong hands, and the young men were caught by them, and not being able to get free, there died a lamentable death.

Many a long year afterwards there came a king's son into that country, and heard an old man tell how there should be a castle standing behind the hedge of thorns, and that there a beautiful enchanted princess named Rosamond had slept for a hundred years, and with her the king and queen, and the whole court. The old man had been told by his grandfather that many kings' sons had sought to pass the thorn-hedge, but had been caught and pierced by the thorns, and had died a miserable death. Then said the young man, "Nevertheless, I do not fear to try; I shall win through and see the lovely Rosamond." The good old man tried to dissuade him, but he would not listen to his words.

For now the hundred years were at an end, and the day had come when Rosamond should be awakened. When the prince drew near the hedge of thorns, it was changed into a hedge of beautiful large flowers, which parted and bent aside to let him pass, and then closed behind him in a thick hedge. When he reached the castle-yard, he saw the horses and brindled hunting-dogs lying asleep, and on the roof the pigeons were sitting with their heads under their wings. And when he came indoors, the flies on the wall were asleep, the cook in the kitchen had his hand uplifted to strike the scullion, and the kitchen-maid had the black fowl on her lap ready to pluck. Then he mounted higher, and saw in the hall the whole court lying asleep, and above them, on their thrones, slept the king and the queen. And still he went farther, and all was so quiet that he could hear his own breathing; and at last he came to the tower, and went up the winding stair, and opened the door of the little room where Rosamond lay. And when he saw her looking so lovely in her sleep, he could not turn away his eyes; and presently he stooped and kissed her, and she awakened, and opened her eyes, and looked very kindly on him. And she rose, and they went forth together, and the king and the queen and whole court woke up, and gazed on each other with great eyes of wonderment. And the horses in the yard got up and shook themselves, the hounds sprang up and wagged their tails, the pigeons on the roof drew their heads from under their wings, looked round, and flew into the field, the flies on the wall crept on a little farther, the kitchen fire leapt up and blazed, and cooked the meat, the joint on the spit began to roast, the cook gave the scullion such a box on the ear that he roared out, and the maid went on plucking the fowl.

Then the wedding of the prince and Rosamond was held with all splendor, and they lived very happily together until their lives' end.

In the old times, when it was still of some use to wish for the thing one wanted, there lived a king whose daughters were all handsome, but the youngest was so beautiful that the sun himself, who has seen so much, wondered each time he shone over her because of her beauty. Near the royal castle there was a great dark wood, and in the wood under an old linden-tree was a well; and when the day was hot, the king's daughter used to go forth into the wood and sit by the brink of the cool well, and if the time seemed long, she would take out a golden ball, and throw it up and catch it again, and this was her favorite pastime.

Now it happened one day that the golden ball, instead of falling back into the maiden's little hand which had sent it aloft, dropped to the ground near the edge of the well and rolled in. The king's daughter followed it with her eyes as it sank, but the well was deep, so deep that the bottom could not be seen. Then she began to weep, and she wept and wept as if she could never be comforted. And in the midst of her weeping she heard a voice saying to her, "What ails thee, king's daughter? thy tears would melt a heart of stone."

And when she looked to see where the voice came from, there was nothing but a frog stretching his thick ugly head out of the water.

"Oh, is it you, old waddler?" said she; "I weep because my golden ball has fallen into the well."

"Never mind, do not weep," answered the frog; "I can help you; but what will you give me if I fetch up your ball again?"

"Whatever you like, dear frog," said she; "any of my clothes, my pearls and jewels, or even the golden crown that I wear."

"Thy clothes, thy pearls and jewels, and thy golden crown are not for me," answered the frog, "but if thou wouldst love me, and have me for thy companion and play-fellow, and let me sit by thee at table, and eat from thy plate, and drink from thy cup, and sleep in thy little bed,—if thou wouldst promise all this, then would I dive below the water and fetch thee thy golden ball again."

"Oh yes," she answered; "I will promise it all, whatever you want, if you only get me my ball again."

But she thought to herself, "What nonsense he talks! as if he could do anything but sit in the water and croak with the other frogs, or could possibly be any one's companion."

But the frog, as soon as he heard her promise, drew his head under the water and sank down out of sight, but after a while he came to the surface again with the ball in his mouth, and he threw it on the grass.

The king's daughter was overjoyed to see her pretty plaything again, and she caught it up and ran off with it.

"Stop, stop!" cried the frog; "take me up too; I cannot run as fast as you!"

But it was of no use, for croak, croak after her as he might, she would not listen to him, but made haste home, and very soon forgot all about the poor frog, who had to betake himself to his well again.

The next day, when the king's daughter was sitting at table with the king and all the court, and eating from her golden plate, there came something pitter patter up the marble stairs, and then there came a knocking at the door, and a voice crying, "Youngest king's daughter, let me in!"

And she got up and ran to see who it could be, but when she opened the door, there was the frog sitting outside. Then she shut the door hastily and went back to her seat, feeling very uneasy. The king noticed how quickly her heart was beating, and said, "My child, what are you afraid of? is there a giant standing at the door ready to carry you away?"

"Oh no," answered she; "no giant, but a horrid frog."

"And what does the frog want?" asked the king.

"O dear father," answered she, "when I was sitting by the well yesterday, and playing with my golden ball, it fell into the water, and while I was crying for the loss of it, the frog came and got it again for me on condition I would let him be my companion, but I never thought that he could leave the water and come after me; but now there he is outside the door, and he wants to come in to me."

And then they all heard him knocking the second time and crying,

> "Youngest king's daughter,
> Open to me!
> By the well water
> What promised you me?
> Youngest king's daughter
> Now open to me!"

"That which thou hast promised must thou perform," said the king; "so go now and let him in."

So she went and opened the door, and the frog hopped in, following at her heels, till she reached her chair. Then he stopped and cried, "Lift me up to sit by you."

But she delayed doing so until the king ordered her. When once the frog was on the chair, he wanted to get on the table, and there he sat and said, "Now push your golden plate a little nearer, so that we may eat together."

And so she did, but everybody might see how unwilling she was, and the frog feasted heartily, but every morsel seemed to stick in her throat.

"I have had enough now," said the frog at last, "and as I am tired, you must carry me to your room, and make ready your silken bed, and we will lie down and go to sleep."

Then the king's daughter began to weep, and was afraid of the cold frog, that nothing would satisfy him but he must sleep in her pretty clean bed. Now the king grew angry with her, saying, "That which thou hast promised in thy time of necessity, must thou now perform."

So she picked up the frog with her finger and thumb, carried him upstairs and put him in a corner, and when she had lain down to sleep, he came creeping up, saying, "I am tired and want sleep as much as you; take me up, or I will tell your father."

Then she felt beside herself with rage, and picking him up, she threw him with all her strength against the wall, crying, "Now will you be quiet, you horrid frog!"

But as he fell, he ceased to be a frog, and became all at once a prince with beautiful kind eyes. And it came to pass that, with her father's consent, they became bride and bridegroom. And he told her how a wicked witch had bound him by her spells, and how no one but she alone could have released him, and that they two would go together to his father's kingdom. And there came to the door a carriage drawn by eight white horses, with white plumes on their heads, and with golden harness, and behind the carriage was standing faithful Henry, the servant of the young prince. Now faithful Henry had suffered such care and pain when his master was turned into a frog, that he had been obliged to wear three iron bands over his heart, to keep it from breaking with trouble and anxiety. When the carriage started to take the prince to his kingdom, and faithful Henry had helped them both in, he got up behind, and was full of joy at his master's deliverance. And when they had gone a part of the way, the prince heard a sound at the back of the carriage, as if something had broken, and he turned round and cried, "Henry, the wheel must be breaking!" but Henry answered,

> "The wheel does not break,
> 'Tis the band round my heart
> That, to lessen its ache,
> When I grieved for your sake,
> I bound round my heart."

Again, and yet once again there was the same sound, and the prince thought it must be the wheel breaking, but it was the breaking of the other bands from faithful Henry's heart, because it was now so relieved and happy.

"What ails thee, king's daughter?" (page 44)

nce after a man and wife had long wished in vain for a child, the wife had reason to hope that God would grant them their wish. In the back of their house there was a little window that looked out over a wonderful garden, full of beautiful flowers and vegetables. But there was a high wall around the garden, and no one dared enter it because it belonged to a witch, who was very powerful and everyone was afraid of her. One day the wife stood at this window, looking down into the garden, and her eyes lit on a bed of the finest rapunzel, which is a kind of lettuce. And it looked so fresh and green that she longed for it and her mouth watered. Her craving for it grew from day to day, and she began to waste away because she knew she would never get any. Seeing her so pale and wretched, her husband took fright and asked: "What's the matter with you, dear wife?" "Oh," she said, "I shall die unless I get some rapunzel to eat from the garden behind our house." Her husband, who loved her, thought: "Sooner than let my wife die, I shall get her some of that rapunzel, cost what it may." As night was falling, he climbed the wall into the witch's garden, took a handful of rapunzel, and brought it to his wife. She made it into a salad right away and ate it hungrily. But it tasted so good, so very good, that the next day her craving for it was three times as great. Her husband could see she would know no peace unless he paid another visit to the garden. So at nightfall he climbed the wall again, but when he came down on the other side he had an awful fright, for there was the witch right in front of him. "How dare you!" she said with an angry look. "How dare you sneak into my garden like a thief and steal my rapunzel! I'll make you pay dearly for this." "Oh, please," he said, "please temper justice with mercy. I only did it because I had to. My wife was looking out of the window, and when she saw your rapunzel she felt such a craving for it that she would have died if I hadn't got her some." At that the witch's anger died down and she said: "If that's how it is, you may take as much rapunzel as you wish, but on one condition: that you give me the child your wife will bear. It will have a good life and I shall care for it like a mother." In his fright, the man agreed to everything, and the moment his wife was delivered, the witch appeared, gave the child the name of Rapunzel, and took her away.

Rapunzel grew to be the loveliest child under the sun. When she was twelve years old, the witch took her to the middle of the forest and shut her up in a tower that had neither stairs nor door, but only a little window at the very top. When the witch wanted to come in, she stood down below and called out:

"Rapunzel, Rapunzel,
Let down your hair for me."

Rapunzel had beautiful long hair, as fine as spun gold. When she heard the witch's voice, she undid her braids and fastened them to the window latch. They fell to the ground twenty ells down, and the witch climbed up on them.

A few years later it so happened that the king's son was passing through the forest. When he came to the tower, he heard someone singing, and the singing was so lovely that he stopped and listened. It was Rapunzel, who in her loneliness was singing to pass the time. The prince wanted to go up to her and he looked for a door but found none. He rode away home, but the singing had so touched his heart that he went out into the forest every day and listened. Once as he was standing behind a tree, he saw a witch come to the foot of the tower and heard her call out:

"Rapunzel, Rapunzel,
Let down your hair."

Whereupon Rapunzel let down her braids, and the witch climbed up to her. "Aha," he thought, "if that's the ladder that goes up to

her, then I'll try my luck too." And next day,
when it was beginning to get dark, he went
to the tower and called out:

"Rapunzel, Rapunzel,
Let down your hair."

A moment later her hair fell to the ground
and the prince climbed up.

At first Rapunzel was dreadfully

frightened, for she had never seen a man before, but the prince spoke gently to her and told her how he had been so moved by her singing that he couldn't rest easy until he had seen her. At that Rapunzel lost her fear, and when he asked if she would have him as her husband and she saw he was young and handsome, she thought: "He will love me better than my old godmother." So she said yes and put her hand in his hand. "I'd gladly go with you," she said, "but how will I ever get down? Every time you come, bring a skein of silk and I'll make a ladder with it. When it's finished, I'll come down, and you will carry me home on your horse." They agreed that in the meantime he would come every evening, because the old witch came during the day. The witch noticed nothing until one day Rapunzel said to her: "Tell me, Godmother, how is it that you're so much harder to pull up than the young prince? With him it hardly takes a minute." "Wicked child!" cried the witch. "What did you say? I thought I had shut you away from the world, but you've deceived me." In her fury she seized Rapunzel's beautiful hair, wound it several times around her left hand and picked up a pair of scissors in her right hand. Snippety-snap went the scissors, and the lovely braids fell to the floor. Then the heartless witch sent Rapunzel to a desert place, where she lived in misery and want.

At dusk on the day she had sent Rapunzel

away, she fastened the severed braids to the window latch, and when the prince came and called:

"Rapunzel, Rapunzel,
Let down your hair."

she let the hair down. The prince climbed up, but instead of his dearest Rapunzel, the witch was waiting for him with angry, poisonous looks. "Aha!" she cried. "You've come to take your darling wife away, but the bird is gone from the nest, she won't be singing any more; the cat has taken her away and before she's done she'll scratch your eyes out too. You've lost Rapunzel, you'll never see her again." The prince was beside himself with grief, and in his despair he jumped from the tower. It didn't kill him, but the brambles he fell into scratched his eyes out and he was blind. He wandered through the forest, living on roots and berries and weeping and wailing over the loss of his dearest wife. For several years he wandered wretchedly, until at last he came to the desert place where Rapunzel was living in misery with the twins she had borne—a boy and a girl. He heard a voice that seemed familiar, and when he approached Rapunzel recognized him, fell on his neck and wept. Two of her tears dropped on his eyes, which were made clear again, so that he could see as well as ever. He took her to his kingdom, where she was welcomed with rejoicing, and they lived happy and contented for many years to come.

here were once a king and a queen who lived together peaceably and had twelve children, who were all boys. One day the king said to his wife: "If the thirteenth child you are about to bear is a girl, the twelve boys must die, so that her wealth may be great and that she alone may inherit the kingdom." He had twelve coffins made and filled with wood shavings, and in each one there was a little pillow. He had them taken to a locked room, gave the queen the key, and told her not to speak of them to anyone.

The mother sat all day and grieved, and her youngest son, who was always with her and whom she called Benjamin, after the Bible, said to her: "Mother dear, why are you so sad?" "Dearest child," she said, "I'm not allowed to tell you." But he gave her no peace until she unlocked the room and showed him the twelve coffins full of wood shavings. Then she said: "Dearest Benjamin, your father has had these coffins made for you and your eleven brothers, for if I give birth to a girl you are all to be killed and buried in them." She wept as she spoke, and her son comforted her, saying: "Don't cry, mother dear, we can take care of ourselves. We'll run away." And she said: "Go to the forest with your eleven brothers. Let each of you by turns climb the highest tree you can find and keep watch. If I give birth to a boy, I shall raise a white flag on this tower, and then you may come back. But if I give birth to a girl, I shall raise a red flag. Then you must escape as fast as you can, and God keep you. Every night I shall get up and pray for you; in the winter I shall pray that you find fire to warm yourselves, and in the summer that you're not wilting in the heat."

When she had given them her blessing, her sons went out into the forest. They took turns watching the tower from the top of the tallest oak tree. When eleven days had passed and it was Benjamin's turn, he saw a flag going up, and it was not the white one but the blood-red one, proclaiming that they should all die. When the brothers heard that, they grew angry and said: "Are we to die on a girl's account? We swear to avenge ourselves. Whenever we meet a girl, her red blood will flow."

Then they went deeper into the forest, and right in the middle where it was darkest they found an enchanted hut that no one was living in. "We will live here," they said, "and you, Benjamin, because you're the youngest and weakest, will stay home and keep house. The rest of us will go out and get food." So they went into the forest and shot hares and deer and birds and pigeons, anything that was good to eat. They brought their kill to Benjamin, who dressed and cooked the meat, and in that way they stilled their hunger. They lived in the hut for ten years, and the time didn't seem long to them.

By then the queen's daughter had grown to be a little girl. She was good of heart and fair of face, and she had a gold star on her forehead. Once when a big washing had been done, she saw twelve men's shirts and asked her mother: "Whom do these shirts belong to? They're much too small for father." Her mother answered with a heavy heart: "Dear child, they belong to your twelve brothers." The little girl said: "Where are my twelve brothers? This is the first I've heard of them." "God only knows where they are," said the queen. "They're out in the world, wandering." Then she took the little girl and unlocked the room and showed her the twelve coffins with the wood shavings and the little pillows in them. "These coffins," she said, "were meant for your brothers, but they secretly went away before you were born." She told her how it had all come about, and the little girl said: "Mother dear, please don't cry. I shall go and look for my brothers."

So she took the twelve shirts and went straight into the big forest. All day she walked and in the evening she came to the enchanted hut. She went in and saw a young boy, who asked her: "Where have you come from and where are you going?" He was amazed to find her so beautiful, dressed like a queen, and with a gold star on her forehead. She answered: "I'm a king's daughter and I'm looking for my twelve brothers, and I shall go on as far as the sky is blue until I find them." And she showed him the twelve shirts that belonged to them. Then Benjamin knew she was his sister and said: "I'm Benjamin, your youngest brother." She wept for joy, and so did Benjamin, and they hugged and kissed each other ever so lovingly. But then he said: "Dear sister, there's still a hitch. Long ago we swore that any girl who crossed our path must die, because we had to leave the kingdom on a girl's account." And she said: "I'll gladly die if that will save my twelve brothers." "No," he said. "I don't want you to die. Sit here under this tub until my eleven brothers come home. I'm sure I can win them over." She did as he had said, and at nightfall the others came home from the hunt. Their supper was ready, and as they sat at the table eating, they asked: "What's new?" "Haven't you heard?" said Benjamin. "No," they replied. "Well," he said, "you've been out in the woods, and I've stayed home; yet I know more than you." "Tell us!" they cried. "Do you promise," he said, "not to kill the first girl who crosses our path?" "Yes!" they all cried. "We shall spare her. Now tell us." Then he said: "Our sister is here!" He lifted up the tub and out came the king's daughter dressed like a queen; she had a gold star on her forehead and was ever so beautiful. They were all overjoyed. They hugged her and kissed her, and loved her with all their hearts.

From then on she stayed in the hut with Benjamin and helped him with his work. The eleven went out into the forest and caught game and deer and birds and pigeons for them to eat, and their sister and Benjamin prepared their meals. She gathered firewood and wild plants and put the pots on the fire, so that supper was always ready when the eleven came home. And she kept the house in order, and made the beds up white and clean, and her brothers were always contented and they lived together in perfect harmony.

One day the two of them prepared a fine meal. When the others came home, they all sat down to eat and drink, and they were full of joy. Now there was a little garden behind the enchanted hut, and in it there were twelve lilies. She wanted to give her brothers pleasure, and so she broke off the flowers, meaning to give one to each of her brothers at supper. But no sooner had she broken off the flowers than her twelve brothers were turned into twelve ravens that flew away over the forest, and in the same moment the hut and garden vanished. The poor girl was left alone in the wilderness, and when she looked around an old woman was standing beside her, who said: "My child, what have you done? Why didn't you leave those twelve flowers alone? They were your brothers, and now they've been turned into ravens forever." The girl wept and said: "Is there no way of saving them?" "No," said the

old woman. "In all the world there's only one way and it's so hard that you can't hope to succeed, for you would have to keep silent for seven years, without speaking and without laughing, and if you said a single word or if a single hour were wanting from the seven years, all your trouble would be in vain, and that one word would kill your brothers."

Then the girl said in her heart: "I know for sure that I'll save my brothers." She picked out a tall tree and climbed up in it, and there she sat spinning, and she neither spoke nor laughed. Now it so happened that a king went hunting in that forest. He had a big greyhound who ran to the tree where the girl was sitting, and he jumped up, yapping and barking. That brought the king to the foot of the tree. He saw the beautiful princess with the gold star on her forehead, and he was so enchanted with her beauty that he called out and asked her if she would like to be his wife. In reply, she said nothing, but she nodded her head a little. So he climbed the tree in person, carried her down, put her on his horse, and took her home. The wedding was celebrated with great splendor and joy, but the bride neither spoke nor laughed. After they had lived happily together for a few years, the king's mother, who was a wicked woman, began to slander the young queen. She said to the king: "That woman you brought home is no better than a beggar. Who knows what godless tricks she's up to!

Even if she's dumb and can't speak, she could laugh once in a while. Anybody who doesn't laugh has a guilty conscience." At first the king refused to believe her, but the old woman kept it up so long and accused her of so many wicked things that the king finally let himself be convinced and condemned her to death.

They made a big fire in the courtyard, and they were going to burn her in it. The king stood at a window and looked down with tears in his eyes, for he still loved her. She was already tied to the stake and the fire was licking at her clothes with red tongues when the last moment of the seven years passed. A whirring was heard, twelve ravens came flying through the air and swooped down. And the moment they touched the ground they became her twelve brothers, for she had saved them. They broke up the fire, put out the flames, set their dear sister free, and hugged her and kissed her. And now that she was able to open her mouth and speak, she told the king why she had kept silent and never laughed. The king was glad to hear she was innocent and they all lived happily together until they died. The wicked step-mother was tried and sentenced and put in a barrel filled with boiling oil and poisonous snakes, and she died a cruel death.

There was once a man whose wife died and a woman whose husband died, and the man had a daughter and the woman also had a daughter. The girls knew each other and went for a walk together and then they went to the woman's house. And the woman said to the man's daughter: "Listen to me. Go and tell your father I want to marry him. Then you will wash in milk every morning and drink wine, but my daughter will wash in water and drink water." The girl went home and told her father what the woman had said. The man said: "What should I do? Marriage is a joy, but it's also torture." Finally, when he couldn't make up his mind, he took off his boot and said: "See this boot? There's a hole in it. Take it up to the attic, hang it on a nail, and pour water into it. If the water stays, I'll take a wife; if it runs out, I won't." The girl did as she was bidden. The water pulled the sides of the hole together and the boot stayed brimful. She told her father what had happened. Then he went up to the attic to see for himself, and when he saw it was true, he went to the widow and courted her, and the wedding was celebrated.

Next morning, when the two girls got up, the husband's daughter had milk to wash in and wine to drink, and the wife's daughter had water to wash in and water to drink. On the second morning, the husband's daughter as well as the wife's daughter had water to wash in and water to drink. On the third morning, the husband's daughter had water to wash in and water to drink, and the wife's daughter had milk to wash in and wine to drink. And that's how it was from then on. The wife hated her stepdaughter like poison and racked her brains looking for ways to make things worse for her from day to day. For one thing, she was envious, because her stepdaughter was beautiful and sweet-tempered, while her own daughter was ugly and horrid.

One winter day, when the ground was frozen solid and hill and dale were covered with snow, the wife made a dress out of paper, called the girl and said: "Put on this dress and go out into the woods. I want you to bring me a little basket full of strawberries. I have a craving for them." "My goodness!" said the girl. "Strawberries don't grow in the wintertime; the ground is frozen and everything is covered with snow. And why do you want me to go out in this paper dress?—it's so cold your breath freezes. The wind will blow through it and the brambles will tear it off me." "Don't you dare talk back to me!" cried the stepmother. "Get a move on and don't show your face again until that basket is full of strawberries." Then she gave her a piece of stale bread. "This will do you for the day," she said. And she thought: "She'll die of cold and hunger out there, and I'll never see her again."

Obediently the stepdaughter put on the paper dress and went out with the little basket. As far as the eye could see, there was nothing but snow, and not the slightest blade of green. When she got to the woods, she saw a hut. Three dwarfs were peering out of it. She bade them good morning and knocked shyly at the door. "Come in!" they cried. She went in and sat down on the bench by the stove to warm herself and eat her breakfast. The dwarfs said: "Give us some." "Gladly," she said, and broke her piece of bread in two and gave them half. "What are you doing out here in the woods in that thin dress in the dead of winter?" they asked. "I've been sent to look for strawberries," she said. "And I'm not to go home until I've picked a basketful." When she had eaten her bread, they gave her a broom and said: "Sweep the snow away from the back door." While she was outside, the three little men talked it over: "What should we give her for being so good and kind and sharing her bread with us?" The first said: "My gift is that she shall become more

beautiful every day." The second said: "My gift is that whenever she says a word a gold piece shall fall out of her mouth." The third said: "My gift is that a king shall come and take her for his wife."

The girl did as the dwarfs had bidden her. She took the broom and swept the snow from behind the hut, and what do you think she found? Ripe strawberries, every one of them dark red, coming up from under the snow. In her joy she picked until her basket was full, thanked the little men, gave each of them her hand, and ran home to bring her stepmother what she had asked for. When she went in and said, "Good evening," a gold piece fell from her mouth. Then she told them what had happened in the woods, and as she spoke the gold pieces kept falling out of her mouth, so that the floor was soon covered with them. "Of all the arrogance!

said her stepsister. "Throwing money around like that!" But in her heart she envied her, and wanted to go out into the woods and look for strawberries. Her mother said: "No, no, my darling daughter, it's too cold, you'd freeze to death." But the daughter gave her no peace, and in the end she let her go. She made her a beautiful fur coat to wear, and gave her sandwiches and cake to take with her.

The girl went to the woods and headed straight for the hut. Again the three dwarfs were peering out, but she didn't say good morning or honor them with so much as a glance. Without a word of greeting she stomped into the hut, sat down by the stove, and began to eat her sandwiches and cake. "Give us some!" the little men cried out, but she replied: "How can I when I haven't enough for myself?" When she had finished eating, they said: "Here's a broom, go and sweep around the back door." "Pooh! Go do your own sweeping," she said. "I'm not your maid." When she saw they weren't going to give her anything, she went outside. The little men talked it over. "What shall we give her for being so horrid and having a wicked, envious heart, and never giving anything away?" The first said: "My gift is that she shall become uglier every day." The second said: "My gift is that whenever she says a word a toad shall jump out of her mouth." The third said: "My gift is that she shall die a cruel death." The girl looked for strawberries outside the hut, and when she didn't find any she went peevishly home. And when she opened her mouth to tell her mother what had happened, a toad jumped out at every word, and everyone thought she was disgusting.

The stepmother was angrier than ever. All she could think of was how to bring sorrow to her husband's daughter, who was growing more beautiful every day. In the end, she took a kettle, put it on the fire, and boiled yarn in it. When the yarn was boiled, she threw it over the poor girl's shoulder, gave her an ax, and told her to go out to the frozen river, cut a hole in the ice and rinse the yarn. Obediently she went to the river and begin to chop a hole in the ice. While she was chopping, a marvelous carriage came along and a king was sitting in it. The carriage stopped and the king asked: "Who are you, my child, and what are you doing here?" "I'm a poor girl and I'm rinsing yarn." The king felt sorry for her, and when he saw how beautiful she was, he said: "Would you like to ride away with me?" "Oh yes, with all my heart," she said, for she was glad to get away from her mother and sister.

So she got into the carriage and rode away with the king, and when they got to his palace their wedding was celebrated with great splendor, and that was the little men's gift to the girl. A year later the young queen gave birth to a son, and when her stepmother heard of her great good fortune, she and her daughter came to the palace as if to pay her a visit. Then one day when the king had gone out and no one else was there, the wicked woman grabbed the queen by the head and her daughter grabbed her by the feet, and they picked her up from her bed and threw her out of the window into the river. Then the ugly daughter lay down in the bed, and the old woman pulled the blankets up over her head. When the king came home and wanted to speak to his wife, the old woman cried: "Hush, hush, not now. She's all in a sweat, you must let her rest." The king thought no harm and didn't come back until the next morning. Then he spoke to his wife and she answered, and at every word a toad jumped out of her mouth, when up until then it had always been a gold piece. He asked what was wrong with her, but the old woman said it came of the bad sweat she'd been in, and the trouble would soon go away.

That night the kitchen boy saw a duck swimming in the runnel, and the duck said:

> "What are you doing, king?
> Are you awake, or slumbering?"

When he didn't answer, the duck said:

> "What are my guests about?"

And the kitchen boy answered:

> "They're sound asleep, no doubt."

Then the duck asked:

"And what of my baby sweet?"

And he answered:

"He's in his cradle asleep."

Then the duck took the form of the queen and went up and suckled the child and plumped up his bed and covered him up. Then she turned into a duck again and swam away in the runnel. Next night she did the same thing, and on the third she said to the kitchen boy: "Go and tell the king to take his sword and stand on the threshold and swing it three times." The kitchen boy ran to the king and told him, and he came with his sword and swung it three times over the ghost. The third time his wife stood before him alive and well and as lovely as ever.

The king was very happy, but he kept the queen hidden in a bedchamber until the Sunday when the child was to be christened. After the christening, the king said: "What should be done to a person who drags some-one out of bed and throws him into the water?" The old woman answered: "The villain should be shut up in a barrel studded with nails and rolled down the hill into the water." The king said: "You've pronounced your own sentence." He sent for just such a barrel, and the old woman and her daughter were put into it, and the lid was hammered tight, and it was rolled down the hill into the river.

ome time ago there reigned in a country many thousands of miles off, an old queen who was very spiteful and delighted in nothing so much as mischief. She had one daughter, who was thought to be the most beautiful princess in the world; but her mother only made use of her as a trap for the unwary; and whenever any suitor who had heard of her beauty came to seek her in marriage, the only answer the old lady gave to each was, that he must undertake some very hard task and forfeit his life if he failed. Many, led by the report of the princess's charms, undertook these tasks, but failed in doing what the queen set them to do. No mercy was ever shown them; but the word was given at once, and off their heads were cut.

Now it happened that a prince who lived in a country far off, heard of the great beauty of this young lady, and said to his father, "Dear father, let me go and try my luck." "No," said the king; "if you go you will surely lose your life." The prince, however, had set his heart so much upon the scheme, that when he found his father was against it he fell very ill, and took to his bed for seven years, and no art could cure him, or recover his lost spirits: so when his father saw that if he went on thus he would die, he said to him with a heart full of grief, "If it must be so, go and try your luck." At this he rose from his bed, recovered his health and spirits, and went forward on his way light of heart and full of joy.

Then on he journeyed over hill and dale, through fair weather and foul, till one day, as he was riding through a wood, he thought he saw afar off some large animal upon the ground, and as he drew near he found that it was a man lying along upon the grass under the trees; but he looked more like a mountain than a man, he was so fat and jolly. When this big fellow saw the traveller, he arose, and said, "If you want any one to wait upon you, you will do well to take me into your service." "What should I do with such a fat fellow as you?" said the prince. "It would be nothing to you if I were three thousand times as fat," said the man, "so that I do but behave myself well." "That's true," answered the prince; "so come with me, I can put you to some use or another I dare say." Then the fat man rose up and followed the prince, and by and by they saw another man lying on the ground with his ear close to the turf. The prince said, "What are you doing there?" "I am listening," answered the man. "To what?" "To all that is going on in the world, for I can

. . . he looked more like a mountain than a man, . . . (page 72)

hear every thing, I can even hear the grass grow." "Tell me," said the prince, "what you hear is going on at the court of the old queen, who has the beautiful daughter?" "I hear," said the listener, "the noise of the sword that is cutting off the head of one of her suitors." "Well!" said the prince, "I see I shall be able to make you of use;—come along with me!" They had not gone far before they saw a pair of feet, and then part of the legs of a man stretched out; but they were so long that they could not see the rest of the body, till they had passed on a good deal farther, and at last they came to the body, and, after going on a while farther, to the head; "Bless me!" said the prince, "what a long rope you are!" "Oh!" answered the tall man, "this is nothing; when I choose to stretch myself to my full length, I am three times as high as any mountain you have seen on your travels, I warrant you; I will willingly do what I can to serve you if you will let me." "Come along then," said the prince, "I can turn you to account in some way."

The prince and his train went on farther into the wood, and next saw a man lying by the road side basking in the heat of the sun, yet shaking and shivering all over, so that not a limb lay still. "What makes you shiver," said the prince, "while the sun is shining so warm?" "Alas!" answered the man, "the warmer it is, the colder I am; the sun only seems to me like a sharp frost that thrills through all my bones; and on the other hand, when others are what you call cold I begin to warm, so that I can neither bear the ice for its heat nor the fire for its cold." "You are a queer fellow," said the prince; "but if you have nothing else to do, come along with me." The next thing they saw was a man standing, stretching his neck and looking around him from hill to hill. "What are you looking for so eagerly?" said the prince. "I have such sharp eyes," said the man, "that I can see over woods and fields and hills and dales;—in short, all over the world." "Well," said the prince, "come with me if you will, for I want one more to make up my train."

Then they all journeyed on, and met with no one else till they came to the city where the beautiful princess lived. The prince went straight to the old queen, and said, "Here I am, ready to do any task you set me, if you will give your daughter as a reward when I have done." "I will set you three tasks," said the queen; "and if you get through all, you shall be the husband of my daughter. First, you must bring me a ring which I dropped in the red sea." The prince went home to his friends and said, "The first task is not an easy one; it is to fetch a ring out of the red sea, so lay your heads together and say what is to be done." Then the sharpsighted one said, "I will see where it lies," and looked down into the sea, and cried out, "There it lies upon a rock at the bottom." "I would fetch it out," said the tall man, "if I could but see it." "Well!" cried out the fat one, "I will help you to do that," and laid himself down and held his mouth to the water, and drank up the waves till the bottom of the sea was as dry as a meadow. Then the tall man stooped a little and pulled out the ring with his hand, and the prince took it to the old queen, who looked at it, and wondering said, "It is indeed the right ring; you have gone through this task well: but now comes the second; look yonder at the meadow before my palace; see! there are a hundred fat oxen feeding there; you must eat them all up before noon: and underneath in my cellar are a hundred casks of wine, which you must drink all up." "May I not invite some guest to share the feast with me?" said the prince. "Why, yes!" said the old woman with a spiteful laugh; "you may ask one of your friends to breakfast with you, but no more."

Then the prince went home and said to the fat man, "You must be my guest to-day, and for once you shall eat your fill." So the fat man set to work and ate the hundred oxen without leaving a bit, and asked if that was to be all he should have for his breakfast? and he drank the wine out of the casks without leaving a drop, licking even his fingers when he had done. When the meal was ended, the prince went to the old woman and told her the second task was done. "Your work is not all over, however," muttered the old hag to herself; "I will catch you yet, you shall not keep your head upon your shoulders if I can help it." "This evening," said she, "I will bring my daughter into your house and leave her with you; you shall sit together there, but take care that you do not fall asleep; for I shall come when the clock strikes twelve, and if she is not then with you, you are undone." "Oh!" thought the prince, "it is an easy task to keep my eyes open." So he called his servants and told them all that the old woman had said. "Who knows though," said he, "but there may be some trick at the bottom of this? it is as well to be upon our guard and keep watch that the young lady does not get away." When it was night the old woman brought her daughter to the prince's house; then the tall man twisted himself round about it, the listener put his ear to the ground, the fat man placed himself before the door so that no living soul could enter, and the sharp-eyed one looked out afar and watched. Within sat the princess without saying a word, but the moon shone bright through the window upon her face, and the prince gazed upon her wonderful beauty. And while he looked upon her with a heart full of joy and love, his eyelids did not droop; but at eleven o'clock the old woman cast a charm over them so that they all fell asleep, and the princess vanished in a moment.

And thus they slept till a quarter to twelve,

when the charm had no longer any power over them, and they all awoke. "Alas! alas! woe is me," cried the prince; "now I am lost for ever." And his faithful servants began to weep over their unhappy lot; but the listener said, "Be still and I will listen;" so he listened a while, and cried out, "I hear her bewailing her fate;" and the sharp-sighted man looked, and said, "I see her sitting on a rock three hundred miles hence; now help us, my tall friend; if you stand up, you will reach her in two steps." "Very well," answered the tall man; and in an instant, before one could turn one's head round, he was at the foot of the enchanted rock. Then the tall man took the young lady in his arms and carried her back to the prince a moment before it struck twelve; and they all sat down again and made merry. And when the clock struck twelve the old queen came sneaking by with a spiteful look, as if she was going to say, "Now he is mine," nor could she think otherwise, for she knew that her daughter was but the moment before on the rock three hundred miles off; but when she came and saw her daughter in the prince's room, she started, and said, "There is somebody here who can do more than I can." However, she now saw that she could no longer avoid giving the prince her daughter for a wife, but said to her in a whisper, "It is a shame that you should be won by servants, and not have a husband of your own choice."

Now the young lady was of a very proud, haughty temper, and her anger was raised to such a pitch, that the next morning she ordered three hundred loads of wood to be brought and piled up; and told the prince it was true he had by the help of his servants done the three tasks, but that before she would marry him some one must sit upon that pile of wood when it was set on fire and bear the heat. She thought to herself that though his servants had done everything else for him, none of them would go so far as to burn themselves for him, and that then she should put his love to the test by seeing whether he would sit upon it himself. But she was mistaken; for when the servants heard this, they said, "We have all done something but the frosty man; now his turn is come," and they took him and put him on the wood and set it on fire. Then the fire rose and burnt for three long days, till all the wood was gone; and when it was out, the frosty man stood in the midst of the ashes trembling like an aspen-leaf, and said, "I never shivered so much in my life; if it had lasted much longer, I should have lost the use of my limbs."

When the princess had no longer any plea for delay, she saw that she was bound to marry the prince; but when they were going to church, the old woman said, "I will never consent;" and sent secret orders out to her horsemen to kill and slay all before them and bring back her daughter before she could be married. However, the listener had pricked up his ears and heard all that the old woman said, and told it to the prince. So they made haste and got to the church first and were married; and then the five servants took their leave and went away saying, "We will go and try our luck in the world on our own account."

The prince set out with his wife, and at the end of the first day's journey came to a village, where a swineherd was feeding his swine; and as they came near he said to his wife, "Do you know who I am? I am not a prince, but a poor swineherd; he whom you see yonder with the swine is my father, and our business will be to help him to tend them." Then he went into the swineherd's hut with her, and ordered her royal clothes to be taken away in the night; so that when she awoke in the morning, she had nothing to put on, till the woman who lived there made a great favour of giving her an old gown and a pair of worsted stockings. "If it were not for your husband's sake," said she, "I would not have given you any thing." Then the poor princess gave herself up for lost, and believed that her husband must indeed be a swineherd; but she thought she would make the best of it, and began to help him to feed them, and said, "It is a just reward for my pride." When this had lasted eight days she could bear it no longer, for her feet were all over wounds, and as she sat down and wept by the way-side, some people came up to her and pitied her, and asked if she knew what her husband really was. "Yes," said she; "a swineherd; he is just gone out to market with some of his stock." But they said, "Come along and we will take you to him," and they took her over the hill to the palace of the prince's father; and when they came into the hall, there stood her husband so richly drest in his royal clothes that she did not know him till he fell upon her neck and kissed her, and said, "I have borne much for your sake, and you too have also borne a great deal for me." Then the guests were sent for, and the marriage feast was given, and all made merry and danced and sung, and the best wish that I can wish is, that you and I had been there too.

Once in midwinter when the snow-flakes were falling from the sky like feathers, a queen sat sewing at a window, with an ebony frame. And as she was sewing and looking out at the snowflakes, she pricked her finger with her needle and three drops of blood fell on the snow. The red looked so beautiful on the white snow that she thought to herself: "If only I had a child as white as snow and as red as blood and as black as the wood of my window frame." A little while later she gave birth to a daughter, who was as white as snow and as red as blood, and her hair was as black as ebony. They called her Snow White, and when she was born, the queen died.

A year later the king took a second wife. She was beautiful, but she was proud and overbearing, and she couldn't bear the thought that anyone might be more beautiful than she. She had a magic mirror, and when she went up to it and looked at herself, she said:

"Mirror, Mirror, here I stand.
Who is the fairest in the land?"

and the mirror answered:

"You, O Queen, are the fairest in the land."

That set her mind at rest, for she knew the mirror told the truth.

But as Snow White grew, she became more and more beautiful, and by the time she was seven years old she was as beautiful as the day and more beautiful than the queen herself. One day when the queen said to her mirror:

"Mirror, Mirror, here I stand.
Who is the fairest in the land?"–

the mirror replied:

"You, O Queen, are the fairest here,
But Snow White is a thousand times more fair."

The queen gasped, and turned yellow and green with envy. Every time she laid eyes on Snow White after that she hated her so much that her heart turned over in her bosom. Envy and pride grew like weeds in her heart, until she knew no peace by day or by night. Finally she sent for a huntsman and said: "Get that child out of my sight. Take her into the forest and kill her and bring me her lungs and her liver to prove you've done it." The huntsman obeyed. He took the child out into the forest, but when he drew his hunting knife and prepared to pierce Snow White's innocent heart, she began to cry and said: "Oh, dear huntsman, let me live. I'll run off through the wild woods and never come home again." Because of her beauty the huntsman took pity on her and said: "All right, you poor child. Run away." To himself, he thought: "The wild beasts will soon eat her," but not having to kill her was a great weight off his mind all the same. Just then a young boar came bounding out of the thicket. The huntsman thrust his knife into it, took the lungs and liver and brought them to the queen as proof that he had done her bidding. The cook was ordered to salt and stew them, and the godless woman ate them, thinking she was eating Snow White's lungs and liver.

Meanwhile the poor child was all alone in the great forest. She was so afraid that she looked at all the leaves on the trees and didn't know what to do. She began to run, she ran over sharp stones and through brambles, and the wild beasts passed by without harming her. She ran as long as her legs would carry her and then, just before nightfall, she saw a little house and went in to rest. Inside the house everything was tiny, but wonderfully neat and clean. There was a table spread with a white cloth, and on the table there were seven little plates, each with its own knife, fork, and spoon, and seven little cups. Over against the wall there were seven little beds all in a row, covered with spotless white sheets. Snow White was very hungry and thirsty, but she didn't want to eat up anyone's entire meal, so she ate a bit of bread and vegetables from each plate and drank a sip of wine from each cup. Then she was so tired that she lay down on one of the beds, but none of the beds quite suited her; some were too long and some were too short, but the seventh was just right. There she stayed and when she had said her prayers she fell asleep.

When it was quite dark, the owners of the little house came home. They were seven dwarfs who went off to the mountains every day with their picks and shovels, to mine silver. They lit their seven little candles, and when the light went up they saw someone had been there, because certain things had been moved. The first said: "Who has been sitting in my chair?" The second: "Who has been eating off my plate?" The third: "Who has taken a bite of my bread?" The fourth: "Who has been eating some of my vegetables?" The fifth: "Who has been using my fork?" The sixth: "Who has been cutting with my knife?" And the seventh: "Who has been drinking out of my cup?" Then the first looked around, saw a little hollow in his bed and said: "Who has been lying in my bed?" The others came running, and cried out: "Somebody has been lying in my bed too." But when the seventh looked at his bed, he saw Snow White lying there asleep. He called the others, who came running. They cried out in amazement, went to get their seven little candles, and held them over Snow White: "Heavens above!" they cried. "Heavens above! What a beautiful child!" They were so delighted they didn't wake her but let her go on sleeping in the little bed. The seventh dwarf slept with his comrades, an hour with each one, and then the night was over.

Next morning Snow White woke up, and when she saw the seven dwarfs she was frightened. But they were friendly and asked: "What's your name?" "My name is Snow White," she said. "How did you get to our house?" the dwarfs asked. And she told them how her stepmother had wanted to kill her, how the huntsman had spared her life, and how she had walked all day until at last she found their little house. The dwarfs said: "If you will keep house for us, and do the cooking and make the beds and wash and sew and knit, and keep everything neat and clean, you can stay with us and you'll want for nothing." "Oh yes," said Snow White. "I'd love to." So she stayed and kept the house in order, and in the morning they went off to the mountains to look for silver and gold, and in the evening they came home again and dinner had to be ready. But all day Snow White was alone, and the kindly dwarfs warned her, saying: "Watch out for your stepmother. She'll soon find out you're here. Don't let anyone in."

After eating Snow White's lungs and liver, the queen felt sure she was again the most beautiful of all. She went to her mirror and said:

"Mirror, Mirror, here I stand.
Who is the fairest in the land?"

And the mirror replied:

"You, O Queen, are the fairest here,

But Snow White, who has gone to stay
With the seven dwarfs far, far away,
Is a thousand times more fair."

The queen gasped. She knew the mirror told
no lies and she realized that the huntsman
had deceived her and that Snow White was
still alive. She racked her brains for a way to
kill her, because she simply had to be the
fairest in the land, or envy would leave her
no peace. At last she thought up a plan. She
stained her face and dressed like an old peddler woman, so that no one could have recognized her. In this disguise she made her
way across the seven mountains to the house
of the seven dwarfs, knocked at the door and
cried out: "Pretty things for sale! For sale!"
Snow White looked out of the window and
said: "Good day, old woman, what have you
got to sell?" "Nice things, nice things!" She
replied. "Laces, all colors," and she took out
a lace woven of bright-colored silk. "This
woman looks so honest," thought Snow
White. "It must be all right to let her in." So
she unbolted the door and bought the pretty
lace. "Child!" said the old woman, "you look
a fright. Come, let me lace you up properly."
Suspecting nothing, Snow White stepped up
and let the old woman put in the new lace.
But she did it so quickly and pulled the lace
so tight that Snow White's breath was cut off
and she fell down as though dead. "Well,
well," said the queen, "you're not the fairest
in the land now." And she hurried away.

A little while later, at nightfall, the seven

dwarfs came home. How horrified they were to see their beloved Snow White lying on the floor! She lay so still they thought she was dead. They lifted her up, and when they saw she was laced too tightly, they cut the lace. She breathed just a little, and then little by little she came to life. When the dwarfs heard what had happened, they said: "That old peddler woman was the wicked queen and no one else. You've got to be careful and never let anyone in when we're away."

When the wicked woman got home, she went to her mirror and asked:

"Mirror, Mirror, here I stand,
Who is the fairest in the land?"

And the mirror answered as usual:

"You, O Queen, are the fairest here,
But Snow White, who has gone to stay
With the seven dwarfs far, far away,
Is a thousand times more fair."

When she heard that, it gave her such a pang that the blood rushed to her heart, for she realized that Snow White had revived. "Never mind," she said. "I'll think up something now that will really destroy you," and with the help of some magic spells she knew she made a poisoned comb. Then she disguised herself and took the form of another old woman. And again she made her way over the seven mountains to the house of the seven dwarfs, knocked at the door and said: "Pretty things for sale! For Sale!" Snow White looked out and said: "Go away. I can't let anyone in." "You can look, can't you?"

said the old woman, taking out the poisoned comb and holding it up. The child liked it so well that she forgot everything else and opened the door. When they had agreed on the price, the old woman said: "Now I'll give your hair a proper combing." Suspecting nothing, poor Snow White stood still for the old woman, but no sooner had the comb touched her hair than the poison took effect and she fell into a dead faint. "There, my beauty," said the wicked woman. "It's all up with you now." And she went away. But luckily it wasn't long till nightfall. When the seven dwarfs came home and found Snow White lying on the floor as though dead, they immediately suspected the stepmother. They examined Snow White and found the poisoned comb, and no sooner had they pulled it out than she woke up and told them what had happened. Again they warned her to be on her guard and not to open the door to anyone.

When the queen got home she went to her mirror and said:

> *"Mirror, Mirror, here I stand.*
> *Who is the fairest in the land?"*

And the mirror answered as before:

> *"You, O Queen, are the fairest here,*
> *But Snow White, who has gone to stay*
> *With the seven dwarfs far, far away,*
> *Is a thousand times more fair."*

When she heard the mirror say that, she trembled and shook with rage. "Snow White must die!" she cried out. "Even if it costs me my own life." Then she went to a secret room that no one else knew about and made a very poisonous apple. It looked so nice on the outside, white with red cheeks, that anyone who saw it would want it; but anyone who ate even the tiniest bit of it would die. When the apple was ready, she stained her face and disguised herself as a peasant woman. And again she made her way across the seven mountains to the house of the seven dwarfs. She knocked at the door and Snow White put her head out of the window. "I can't let anyone in," she said. "The seven dwarfs won't let me." "It doesn't matter," said the peasant woman. "I only want to get rid of these apples. Here. I'll make you a present of one." "No," said Snow White. "I'm not allowed to take anything." "Are you afraid of poison?" said the old woman. "Look, I'm cutting it in half. You eat the red cheek and I'll eat the white cheek." But the

apple had been so cleverly made that only the red cheek was poisoned. Snow White longed for the lovely apple, and when she saw the peasant woman taking a bite out of it she couldn't resist. She held out her hand and took the poisonous half. And no sooner had she taken a bite than she fell to the floor dead. The queen gave her a cruel look, laughed a terrible laugh, and said: "White as snow, red as blood, black as ebony. The dwarfs won't revive you this time." And when she got home and questioned the mirror:

> *"Mirror, Mirror, here I stand,*
> *Who is the fairest in the land?"*

the mirror answered at last:

> *"You, O Queen, are the fairest in the land."*

Then her envious heart was at peace, insofar as an envious heart can be at peace.

When the dwarfs came home at nightfall, they found Snow White lying on the floor. No breath came out of her mouth and she was really dead. They lifted her up, looked to see if they could find anything poisonous, unlaced her, combed her hair, washed her in water and wine, but nothing helped; the dear child was dead, and dead she remained. They laid her on a bier, and all seven sat down beside it and mourned, and they wept for three whole days. Then they were going to bury her, but she still looked fresh and alive, and she still had her beautiful red cheeks. "We can't lower her into the black earth," they said, and they had a coffin made out of glass, so that she could be seen from all sides, and they put her into it and wrote her name in gold letters on the coffin, adding that she was a king's daughter. Then they put the coffin on the hilltop, and one of them always stayed there to guard it. And the birds came and wept for Snow White, first an owl, then a raven, and then a dove.

Snow White lay in her coffin for years and years. She didn't rot, but continued to look as if she were asleep, for she was still as white as snow, as red as blood, and as black as ebony. Then one day a prince came to that forest and stopped for the night at the dwarfs' house. He saw the coffin on the hilltop, he saw lovely Snow White inside it, and he read the gold letters on the coffin. He said to the dwarfs: "Let me have the coffin, I'll pay you as much as you like for it." But the dwarfs replied: "We wouldn't part with it for all the money in the world." "Then give it to me," he said, "for I can't go on living unless I look at Snow White. I will honor and cherish her forever." Then the dwarfs took pity on him and gave him the coffin. The prince's servants hoisted it up on their shoulders and as they were carrying it away they stumbled over a root. The jolt shook the poisoned core, which Snow White had bitten off, out of her throat, and soon she opened her eyes, lifted the coffin lid, sat up, and was alive again. "Oh!" she cried. "Where am I?" "With me!" the prince answered joyfully. Then he told her what had happened and said: "I love you more than anything in the world; come with me to my father's castle and be my wife." Snow White loved him and went with him, and arrangements were made for a splendid wedding feast.

Snow White's wicked stepmother was among those invited to the wedding. When she had put on her fine clothes, she went to her mirror and said:

> "Mirror, Mirror, here I stand,
> Who is the fairest in the land?"

And the mirror answered:

> "You, O Queen, are the fairest here,
> But the young queen is a thousand times more fair."

At that the wicked woman spat out a curse. She was so horror-stricken she didn't know what to do. At first she didn't want to go to the wedding, but then she couldn't resist; she just had to go and see the young queen. The moment she entered the hall she recognized Snow White, and she was so terrified that she just stood there and couldn't move. But two iron slippers had already been put into glowing coals. Someone took them out with a pair of tongs and set them down in front of her. She was forced to step into the red-hot shoes and dance till she fell to the floor dead.

here was once a queen and she had a little daughter, who was as yet a babe in arms; and once the child was so restless that the mother could get no peace, do what she would; so she lost patience, and seeing a flight of ravens passing over the castle, she opened the window and said to her child, "Oh, that thou wert a raven and couldst fly away, that I might be at peace."

No sooner had she uttered the words, than the child was indeed changed into a raven, and fluttered from her arms out of the window. And she flew into a dark wood and stayed there a long time, and her parents knew nothing of her. Once a man was passing through the wood, and he heard the raven cry, and he followed the voice; and when he came near it said, "I was born a king's daughter, and have been bewitched, but thou canst set me free."

"What shall I do?" asked the man.

"Go deeper into the wood," said she, "and thou shalt find a house and an old woman sitting in it: she will offer thee meat and drink, but thou must take none; if thou eatest or drinkest thou fallest into a deep sleep, and canst not set me free at all. In the garden behind the house is a big heap of tan, stand upon that and wait for me. Three days, at about the middle of the day, shall I come to thee in a car drawn by four white horses the first time, by four red ones the second time, and lastly by four black ones; and if thou art not waking but sleeping, thou failest to set me free."

The man promised to do all she said.

"But ah!" cried she, "I know quite well I shall not be set free of thee; something thou wilt surely take from the old woman."

But the man promised yet once more that certainly he would not touch the meat or the drink. But when he came to the house the old woman came up to him.

"My poor man," said she to him, "you are quite tired out, come and be refreshed, and eat and drink."

"No," said the man, "I will eat and drink nothing."

But she left him no peace, saying, "Even if you eat nothing, take a draught out of this cup once and away."

So he was over-persuaded, and he drank.

In the afternoon, about two o'clock, he went out into the garden to stand upon the tan-heap and wait for the raven. As he stood there he felt all at once so tired, that he could bear it no longer, and laid himself down for a little; but not to sleep. But no sooner was he stretched at length than his eyes closed of themselves, and he fell asleep, and slept so sound, as if nothing in the world could awaken him.

At two o'clock came the raven in the car drawn by four white horses, but she was sad, knowing already that the man would be asleep, and so, when she came into the garden, there he lay sure enough. And she got out of the car and shook him and called to him, but he did not wake. The next day at noon the old woman came and brought him meat and drink, but he would take none. But she left him no peace, and persuaded him until he took a draught out of the cup. About two o'clock he went into the garden to stand upon the tan-heap, and to wait for the raven, but he was overcome with so great a weariness that his limbs would no longer hold him up; and whether he would or no he had to lie down, and he fell into a deep sleep. And when the raven came up with her four red horses, she was sad, knowing already that the man would be asleep. And she went up to him, and there he lay, and nothing would wake him.

The next day the old woman came and asked what was the matter with him, and if he wanted to die, that he would neither eat nor drink; but he answered, "I neither can nor will eat and drink."

But she brought the dishes of food and the cup of wine, and placed them before him, _____ and when the smell came in his nostrils he could not refrain, but took a deep draught. When the hour drew near, he went into the garden and stood on the tan-heap to wait for the king's daughter; as time went on he grew more and more weary, and at last he laid himself down and slept like a stone. At two o'clock came the raven with four black horses, and the car and all was black; and she was sad, knowing already that he was sleeping, and would not be able to set her free; and when she came up to him, there he lay and slept. She shook him and called to him, but she could not wake him. Then she laid a loaf by his side and some meat, and a flask of wine, for now, however much he ate and drank, it could not matter. And she took a ring of gold from her finger, and put it on his finger, and her name was engraved on it. And lastly she laid by him a letter, in which was set down what she had given him, and that all was of no use, and further also it said, "I see that here thou canst not save me, but if thy mind is to the thing, come to the golden castle of Stromberg: I know well that if thou willst thou canst." And when all this was done, she got again into her car, and went to the golden castle of Stromberg.

When the man woke up and perceived that he had been asleep, he was sad at heart to think that she had been, and gone, and that he had not set her free. Then, catching sight of what lay beside him, he read the letter that told him all. And he rose up and

Then the giant bore the man . . . (page 99)

set off at once to go to the golden castle of Stromberg, though he knew not where it was. And when he had wandered about in the world for a long time, he came to a dark wood, and there spent a fortnight trying to find the way out, and not being able. At the end of this time, it being towards evening, he was so tired that he laid himself down under a clump of bushes and went to sleep. The next day he went on again, and in the evening, when he was going to lie down again to rest, he heard howlings and lamentations, so that he could not sleep. And about the hour when lamps are lighted, he looked up and saw a light glimmer in the forest; and he got up and followed it, and he found that it came from a house that looked very small indeed, because there stood a giant before it. And the man thought to himself that if he were to try to enter and the giant were to see him, it would go hard and he should lose his life. At last he made up his mind, and walked in. And the giant saw him.

"I am glad thou art come," said he; "it is now a long time since I have had anything to eat; I shall make a good supper of thee."

"That may be," said the man, "but I shall not relish it; besides, if thou desirest to eat, I have somewhat here that may satisfy thee."

"If that is true," answered the giant, "thou mayest make thy mind easy; it was only for want of something better that I wished to devour thee."

Then they went in and placed themselves

at the table, and the man brought out bread, meat, and wine in plenty.

"This pleases me well," said the giant, and he ate to his heart's content. After a while the man asked him if he could tell him where the golden castle of Stromberg was.

"I will look on my land-chart," said the giant, "for on it all towns and villages and houses are marked."

So he fetched the land-chart which was in his room, and sought for the castle, but it was not to be found.

"Never mind," said he, "I have up-stairs in the cupboard much bigger maps than this; we will have a look at them." And so they did, but in vain.

And now the man wanted to pursue his journey, but the giant begged him to stay a few days longer, until his brother, who had gone to get in a store of provisions, should return. When the brother came, they asked him about the golden castle of Stromberg.

"When I have had time to eat a meal and be satisfied, I will look at the map."

That being done, he went into his room with them, and they looked at his maps, but could find nothing: then he fetched other old maps, and they never left off searching until they found the golden castle of Stromberg, but it was many thousand miles away.

"How shall I ever get there?" said the man.

"I have a couple of hours to spare," said

the giant, "and I will set you on your way, but I shall have to come back and look after the child that we have in the house with us."

Then the giant bore the man until within about a hundred hours' journey from the castle, and saying, "You can manage the rest of the way by yourself," he departed; and the man went on day and night, until at last he came to the golden castle of Stromberg. It stood on a mountain of glass, and he could see the enchanted princess driving round it, and then passing inside the gates. He was rejoiced when he saw her, and began at once to climb the mountain to get to her; but it was so slippery, as fast as he went he fell back again. And when he saw this he felt he should never reach her, and he was full of grief, and resolved at least to stay at the foot of the mountain and wait for her. So he built himself a hut, and sat there and waited a whole year; and every day he saw the princess drive round and pass in, and was never able to reach her.

One day he looked out of his hut and saw three robbers fighting, and he called out, "Mercy on us!" Hearing a voice, they stopped for a moment, but went on again beating one another in a dreadful manner. And he cried out again, "Mercy on us!" They stopped and listened, and looked about them, and then went on again. And he cried out a third time, "Mercy on us!" and then, thinking he would go and see what was the matter, he went out and asked them what they were fighting for. One of them told him he had found a stick which would open any door only by knocking at it; the second said he had found a cloak which, if he put it on, made him invisible; the third said he was possessed of a horse that would ride over everything, even the glass mountain. Now they had fought because they could not agree whether they should enjoy these things in common or separately.

"Suppose we make a bargain," said the man; "it is true I have no money, but I have other things yet more valuable to exchange for these; I must, however, make trial of them beforehand, to see if you have spoken truth concerning them."

So they let him mount the horse, and put the cloak round him, and they gave him the stick into his hand, and as soon as he had all this he was no longer to be seen; but laying about him well, he gave them all a sound thrashing, crying out, "Now, you good-for-nothing fellows, you have got what you deserve; perhaps you will be satisfied now!"

Then he rode up the glass mountain, and when he reached the castle gates he found them locked; but he beat with his stick upon the door and it opened at once. And he walked in, and up the stairs to the great room where sat the princess with a golden cup and wine before her: she could not see him so long as the cloak was on him, but drawing near to her he pulled off the ring she had given him, and threw it into the cup with a clang.

"This is my ring," she cried, "and the man who is to set me free must be here too!"

But though she sought through the whole castle she found him not; he had gone outside, seated himself on his horse, and thrown off the cloak. And when she came to look out at the door, she saw him and shrieked out for joy; and he dismounted and took her in his arms, and she kissed him, saying, "Now has thou set me free from my enchantment, and to-morrow we will be married."

here was once a man who was a Jack-of-all-trades; he had served in the war, and had been brave and bold, but at the end of it he was sent about his business, with three farthings and his discharge.

"I am not going to stand this," said he; "wait till I find the right man to help me, and the king shall give me all the treasures of his kingdom before he has done with me."

Then, full of wrath, he went into the forest, and he saw one standing there by six trees which he had rooted up as if they had been stalks of corn. And he said to him, "Will you be my man, and come along with me?"

"All right," answered he; "I must just take this bit of wood home to my father and mother." And taking one of the trees, he bound it round the other five, and putting the faggot on his shoulder, he carried it off; then soon coming back, he went along with his leader, who said, "Two such as we can stand against the whole world."

And when they had gone on a little while, they came to a huntsman who was kneeling on one knee and taking careful aim with his rifle.

"Huntsman," said the leader, "what are you aiming at?"

"Two miles from here," answered he, "there sits a fly on the bough of an oak tree, I mean to put a bullet into its left eye."

"Oh, come along with me," said the leader; "three of us together can stand against the world."

The huntsman was quite willing to go with him, and so they went on till they came to seven windmills, whose sails were going round briskly, and yet there was no wind blowing from any quarter, and not a leaf stirred.

"Well," said the leader, "I cannot think what ails the windmills, turning without wind;" and he went on with his followers about two miles farther, and then they came to a man sitting up in a tree, holding one nostril and blowing with the other.

"Now then," said the leader, "what are you doing up there?"

"Two miles from here," answered he, "there are seven windmills; I am blowing, and they are going round."

"Oh, go with me," cried the leader, "four of us together can stand against the world."

So the blower got down and went with them, and after a time they came to a man standing on one leg, and the other had been taken off and was lying near him.

"You seem to have got a handy way of resting yourself," said the leader to the man.

"I am a runner," answered he, "and in order to keep myself from going too fast I have taken off a leg, for when I run with both, I go faster than a bird can fly."

"Oh, go with me," cried the leader, "five of us together may well stand against the world."

So he went with them all together, and it was not long before they met a man with a little hat on, and he wore it just over one ear.

"Manners! manners!" said the leader; "with your hat like that, you look like a jack-fool."

"I dare not put it straight," answered the other; "if I did, there would be such a terrible frost that the very birds would be frozen and fall dead from the sky to the ground."

"Oh, come with me," said the leader; "we six together may well stand against the whole world."

So the six went on until they came to a town where the king had caused it to be made known that whoever would run a race with his daughter and win it might become her husband, but that whoever lost must lose his head into the bargain. And the leader came forward and said one of his men should run for him.

"Then," said the king, "his life too must be put in pledge, and if he fails, his head and yours too must fall."

When this was quite settled and agreed

upon, the leader called the runner, and strapped his second leg on to him.

"Now, look out," said he, "and take care that we win."

It had been agreed that the one who should bring water first from a far distant brook should be accounted winner. Now the king's daughter and the runner each took a pitcher, and they started both at the same time; but in one moment, when the king's daughter had gone but a very little way, the runner was out of sight, for his running was as if the wind rushed by. In a short time he reached the brook, filled his pitcher full of water, and turned back again. About half-way home, however, he was overcome with weariness, and setting down his pitcher, he lay down on the ground to sleep. But in order to awaken soon again by not lying too soft he had taken a horse's skull which lay near and placed it under his head for a pillow. In the meanwhile the king's daughter, who really was a good runner, good enough to beat an ordinary man, had reached the brook, and filled her pitcher, and was hastening with it back again, when she saw the runner lying asleep.

"The day is mine," said she with much joy, and she emptied his pitcher and hastened on. And now all had been lost but for the huntsman who was standing on the castle wall, and with his keen eyes saw all that happened.

"We must not be outdone by the king's

daughter," said he, and he loaded his rifle and took so good an aim that he shot the horse's skull from under the runner's head without doing him any harm. And the runner awoke and jumped up, and saw his pitcher standing empty and the king's daughter far on her way home. But, not losing courage, he ran swiftly to the brook, filled it again with water, and for all that, he got home ten minutes before the king's daughter.

"Look you," said he; "this is the first time I have really stretched my legs; before it was not worth the name of running."

The king was vexed, and his daughter yet more so, that she should be beaten by a discharged common soldier; and they took counsel together how they might rid themselves of him and of his companions at the same time.

"I have a plan," said the king; "do not fear

but that we shall be quit of them for ever." Then he went out to the men and bade them to feast and be merry and eat and drink; and he led them into a room, which had a floor of iron, and the doors were iron, the windows had iron frames and bolts; in the room was a table set out with costly food.

"Now, go in there and make yourselves comfortable," said the king.

And when they had gone in, he had the door locked and bolted. Then he called the cook, and told him to make a big fire underneath the room, so that the iron floor of it should be red hot. And the cook did so, and the six men began to feel the room growing very warm, by reason, as they thought at first, of the good dinner; but as the heat grew greater and greater, and they found the doors and windows fastened, they began to think it was an evil plan of the king's to suffocate them.

"He shall not succeed, however," said the man with the little hat; "I will bring on a frost that shall make the fire feel ashamed of itself, and creep out of the way."

So he set his hat straight on his head, and immediately there came such a frost that all the heat passed away and the food froze in the dishes. After an hour or two had passed, and the king thought they must have all perished in the heat, he caused the door to be opened, and went himself to see how they fared. And when the door flew back, there they were all six quite safe and sound, and they said they were quite ready to come out, so that they might warm themselves, for the great cold of that room had caused the food to freeze in the dishes. Full of wrath, the king went to the cook and scolded him, and asked why he had not done as he was ordered.

"It is hot enough there: you may see for yourself," answered the cook. And the king looked and saw an immense fire burning underneath the room of iron, and he began to think that the six men were not to be got rid of in that way. And he thought of a new plan by which it might be managed, so he sent for the leader and said to him, "If you will give up your right to my daughter, and take gold instead, you may have as much as you like."

"Certainly, my lord king," answered the man; "let me have as much gold as my servant can carry, and I give up all claim to your daughter." And the king agreed that he should come again in a fortnight to fetch the gold. The man then called together all the tailors in the kingdom, and set them to work to make a sack, and it took them a fortnight. And when it was ready, the strong man who had been found rooting up trees took it on his shoulder, and went to the king.

"Who is this immense fellow carrying on his shoulder a bundle of stuff as big as a house?" cried the king, terrified to think how much gold he would carry off. And a ton of gold was dragged in by sixteen strong men, but he put it all into the sack with one hand, saying, "Why don't you bring some more? this hardly covers the bottom!" So the king bade them fetch by degrees the whole of his treasure, and even then the sack was not half full.

"Bring more!" cried the man; "these few scraps go no way at all!" Then at last seven thousand wagons laden with gold collected through the whole kingdom were driven up; and he threw them in his sack, oxen and all.

"I will not look too closely," said he, "but take what I can get, so long as the sack is full." And when all was put in there was still plenty of room.

"I must make an end of this," he said; "if it is not full, it is so much the easier to tie up." And he hoisted it on his back, and went off with his comrades.

When the king saw all the wealth of his realm carried off by a single man he was full of wrath, and he bade his cavalry mount, and follow after the six men, and take the sack away from the strong man.

Two regiments were soon up to them, and called them to consider themselves prisoners, and to deliver up the sack, or be cut in pieces.

"Prisoners, say you?" said the man who could blow, "suppose you first have a little dance together in the air," and holding one nostril, and blowing through the other, he sent the regiments flying head over heels, over the hills and far away. But a sergeant who had nine wounds and was a brave fellow, begged not to be put to so much shame. And the blower let him down easily, so that he came to no harm, and he bade him go to the king and tell him that whatever regiments he liked to send more should be blown away just the same. And the king, when he got the message, said, "Let the fellows be; they have some right on their side." So the six comrades carried home their treasure, divided it among them, and lived contented till they died.

 king had a daughter who was beautiful beyond measure, but so proud and overbearing that none of her suitors were good enough for her; she not only refused one after the other, but made a laughing-stock of them. Once the king appointed a great feast, and bade all the marriageable men to it from far and near. And they were all put in rows, according to their rank and station; first came the kings, then the princes, the dukes, the earls, the barons, and lastly the noblemen. The princess was led in front of the rows, but she had a mocking epithet for each. One was too fat, "What a tub!" said she. Another too tall, "Long and lean is ill to be seen," said she. A third too short, "Fat and short not fit to court," said she. A fourth was too pale, "A regular death's-head;" a fifth too red-faced, "A game-cock," she called him. The sixth was not well-made enough, "Green wood ill dried!" cried she. So every one had something against him, and she made especially merry over a good king who was very tall, and whose chin had grown a little peaked.

"Only look," cried she, laughing, "he has a chin like a thrush's beak."

And from that time they called him King Thrushbeard. But the old king, when he saw that his daughter mocked every one, and scorned all the assembled suitors, swore in his anger that she should have the first beggar that came to the door for a husband.

A few days afterwards came a travelling ballad singer, and sang under the window in hopes of a small alms. When the king heard of it, he said that he must come in. And so the ballad singer entered in his dirty tattered garments, and sang before the king and his daughter; when he had done, he asked for a small reward. But the king said, "Thy song has so well pleased me, that I will give thee my daughter to wife."

The princess was horrified; but the king said, "I took an oath to give you to the first beggar that came, and so it must be done."

There was no remedy. The priest was fetched, and she had to be married to the ballad-singer out of hand. When all was done, the king said, "Now, as you are a beggar-wife, you can stay no longer in my castle, so off with you and your husband."

The beggar-man led her away, and she was obliged to go forth with him on foot. On the way they came to a great wood, and she asked,

"Oh, whose is this forest, so thick and so fine?"

He answered,

"It is King Thrushbeard's, and might have been thine."

And she cried,

"Oh. I was a silly young thing, I'm afeared,
Would I had taken that good King Thrushbeard!"

Then they passed through a meadow, and she asked,

"Oh, whose is this meadow, so green and so fine?"

He answered,

"It is King Thrushbeard's, and might have been thine."

And she cried.

"I was a silly young thing, I'm afeared,
Would I had taken that good King Thrushbeard!"

Then they passed through a great town, and she asked,

"Whose is this city, so great and so fine?"

He answered,

"Oh, it is King Thrushbeard's, and might have been thine."

And she cried,

"I was a silly young thing, I'm afeared,
Would I had taken that good King Thrushbeard!"

Then said the beggar-man, "It does not please me to hear you always wishing for another husband; am I not good enough for you?"

At last they came to a very small house, and she said,

"Oh dear me! what poor little house do I see?
And whose, I would know, may the wretched hole be?"

The man answered,
"That is my house and thine, where we must live together."

She had to stoop before she could go in at the door.

"Where are the servants?" asked the king's daughter.

"What servants?" answered the beggar-man, "what you want to have done you must do yourself. Make a fire quick, and put on water, and cook me some food; I am very tired."

But the king's daughter understood nothing about fire-making and cooking, and the beggar-man had to lend a hand himself in order to manage it at all. And when they had eaten their poor fare, they went to bed; but the man called up his wife very early in the morning, in order to clean the house. For a few days they lived in this indifferent manner, until they came to the end of their store.

"Wife," said the man, "this will not do, stopping here and earning nothing; you must make baskets."

So he went out and cut willows, and brought them home; and she began to weave them, but the hard twigs wounded her tender hands.

"I see this will not do," said the man, "you had better try spinning."

So she sat her down and tried to spin, but the harsh thread cut her soft fingers, so that the blood flowed.

"Look now!" said the man, "you are no good at any sort of work; I made a bad bargain when I took you. I must see what I can do to make a trade of pots and earthen vessels; you can sit in the market and offer them for sale."

"Oh dear!" thought she, "suppose while I am selling in the market people belonging to my father's kingdom should see me, how they would mock at me!"

But there was no help for it; she had to submit, or else die of hunger.

The first day all went well; the people bought her wares eagerly, because she was so beautiful, and gave her whatever she asked, and some of them gave her the money and left the pots after all behind them. And they lived on these earnings as long as they lasted; and then the man bought a number of new pots. So she seated herself in a corner of the market, and stood the wares before her for sale. All at once a drunken horse-soldier came plunging by, and rode straight into the midst of her pots, breaking them into a thousand pieces. She could do nothing for weeping.

"Oh dear, what will become of me," cried she; "what will my husband say?" and she hastened home and told him her misfortune.

"Who ever heard of such a thing as sitting in the corner of the market with earthenware pots!" said the man; "now leave off crying; I see you are not fit for any regular work. I have been asking at your father's castle if they want a kitchenmaid, and they say they don't mind taking you; at any rate you will get your victuals free."

kitchen-maid, to be at the cook's beck and call, and to do the hardest work. In each of her pockets she fastened a little pot, and brought home in them whatever was left, and upon that she and her husband were fed. It happened one day, when the wedding of the eldest prince was celebrated, the poor woman went upstairs, and stood by the parlor door to see what was going on. And when the place was lighted up, and the company arrived, each person handsomer than the one before, and all was brilliancy and splendor, she thought on her own fate with a sad heart, and bewailed her former pride and the haughtiness which had brought her so low, and plunged her in so great poverty. And as the rich and delicate dishes smelling so good were carried to and fro every now and then, the servants would throw her a few fragments, which she put in her pockets, intending to take home. And then the prince himself passed, clothed in silk and velvet, with a gold chain round his neck. And when he saw the beautiful woman standing in the doorway, he seized her hand and urged her to dance with him, but she refused, all trembling, for she saw it was King Thrushbeard, who had come to court her, whom she had turned away with mocking. It was of no use her resisting, he drew her into the room; and all at once the band to which her pockets were fastened broke, and the pots fell out, and the soup ran about, and the

fragments were scattered all round. And when the people saw that, there was great laughter and mocking, and she felt so ashamed, that she wished herself a thousand fathoms underground. She rushed to the door to fly from the place, when a man caught her just on the steps, and when she looked at him, it was King Thrushbeard again. He said to her in a kind tone, "Do not be afraid, I and the beggar-man with whom you lived in the wretched little hut are one. For love of you I disguised myself, and it was I who broke your pots in the guise of a horse-soldier. I did all that to bring down your proud heart, and to punish your haughtiness, which caused you to mock at me." Then she wept bitterly, and said, "I have done great wrong, and am not worthy to be your wife."

But he said, "Take courage, the evil days

are gone over; now let us keep our wedding-day."

Then came the ladies-in-waiting and put on her splendid clothing; and her father came, and the whole court, and wished her joy on her marriage with King Thrushbeard; and then the merry-making began in good earnest. I cannot help wishing that you and I could have been there too.

here was once an old castle in a great dense forest; an old woman lived there all by herself and she was a wicked witch. In the daytime she turned herself into a cat or a night owl, but at night she resumed her human form. She had a way of luring birds and game, and when she had killed them, she would boil or roast them. If anyone came within a hundred steps of the castle, they froze in their tracks and couldn't stir from the spot until she said certain words that broke the spell. If an innocent girl went inside the circle, the witch turned her into a bird and shut her up in a wicker cage, which she carried to one of the rooms in her castle. She had about seven thousand of these rare birds, all in wicker cages.

Now there was once a girl named Jorinda, who was more beautiful than all the other girls in the world. She was betrothed to a handsome boy named Joringel. They were planning to marry soon and their greatest joy was in being together. One afternoon, wanting to be alone and undisturbed, they went into the forest. "Take care," said

Joringel, "don't go too near the castle." It was a lovely evening; the sun shone between the tree trunks and lit up the dark green darkness of the forest, and the turtledoves sang mournfully in the old beech trees.

Now and then Jorinda wept. She sat down in the sun and sighed, and Joringel sighed too. They were as sad as if death had been near. They looked around in bewilderment, for they no longer knew the way home. The sun was still half above the hill and half below it. Joringel looked through the bushes and saw the old castle wall only a few steps away. He was overcome with horror and dread. Jorinda sang:

> *"My little bird with the ring so red*
> *Sings sorrow, sorrow, sorrow;*
> *he sings that the turtledove is dead,*
> *sings sorrow, sor— jug, jug, jug."*

Joringel looked at Jorinda. She had been turned into a nightingale and was singing "jug jug jug." A night owl with fiery eyes flew around her three times and screeched three times: "To whoo, to whoo, to whoo." Joringel couldn't move, he stood as still as a stone, unable to weep, to speak, to move hand or foot. The sun had gone down; the owl flew into a bush; a moment later a gnarled old woman, yellow and scrawny, came out of it. She had big red eyes and a crooked nose, the end of which touched her chin. Muttering to herself, she caught the nightingale in her hands and carried it away.

She had a way of luring birds and game, . . . (page 119)

Joringel couldn't say a word or stir from the spot, and the nightingale was gone. At last the woman came back and said in a muffled voice: "Greetings, Zachiel! When the moon shines on the cage, let him go." And Joringel was free. He fell on his knees and begged the old woman to give him back his Jorinda, but she said he would never see her again and left him. He cried out, he wept, he moaned, but all in vain. "Oh! Oh! What's to become of me?" Joringel went away and came at last to a strange village, and stayed there a long time guarding the sheep. He often walked around the castle, but not too close. Then one night he dreamed he had found a blood-red flower with a fine large pearl in it. He plucked the flower and went to the castle with it. Everything he touched with the flower was freed from the spell. He also dreamed that the flower helped him get his Jorinda back again.

When he woke up the next morning, he began to search hill and dale for the flower; eight days he searched and early in the morning of the ninth he found the blood-red flower. In the middle there was a big dewdrop, as big as the finest pearl. Holding the flower, he journeyed day and night until he reached the castle. When he came to within a hundred paces of the castle, he was not held fast, but continued on to the gate. His heart leaped. He touched the gate with the flower, and it sprang open. He went in, passed through the courtyard, and listened for the sound of the birds. At length he heard them. On and on he went till he found the room, and there was the witch feeding the birds in the seven thousand cages. When she saw Joringel, she was angry, very angry; she scolded, she spat poison and gall at him, but she couldn't get near him, not within two paces. Paying no attention to her, he went up and down the room looking at the birds in the cages, but there were hundreds of nightingales: how was he ever to find his Jorinda? Suddenly, while he was watching the birds, he saw the old witch taking a cage down on the sly and making for the door with it. In a flash he jumped and touched the cage with the flower. He also touched the old woman and she lost her power to work magic. And there stood Jorinda with her arms around his neck, as beautiful as ever. After turning all the other birds back into girls, he went home with his Jorinda, and they lived happily together for many years.

A widow had two daughters; one was pretty and industrious, the other was ugly and lazy. And as the ugly one was her own daughter, she loved her much the best, and the pretty one was made to do all the work, and be the drudge of the house. Every day the poor girl had to sit by a well on the high road and spin until her fingers bled. Now it happened once that as the spindle was bloody, she dipped it into the well to wash it; but it slipped out of her hand and fell in. Then she began to cry, and ran to her stepmother, and told her of her misfortune; and her stepmother scolded her without mercy, and said in her rage, "As you have let the spindle fall in, you must go and fetch it out again!"

Then the girl went back to the well, not knowing what to do, and in the despair of her heart she jumped down into the well the same way the spindle had gone. After that she knew nothing; and when she came to herself she was in a beautiful meadow, and the sun was shining on the flowers that grew round her. And she walked on through the meadow until she came to a baker's oven that was full of bread; and the bread called out to her, "Oh, take me out, take me out, or I shall burn; I am baked enough already!"

Then she drew near, and with the baker's peel she took out all the loaves one after the other. And she went farther on till she came to a tree weighed down with apples, and it called out to her, "Oh, shake me, shake me, we apples are all of us ripe!"

Then she shook the tree until the apples fell like rain, and she shook until there were no more to fall; and when she had gathered them together in a heap, she went on farther. At last she came to a little house, and an old woman was peeping out of it, but she had such great teeth that the girl was terrified and about to run away, only the old woman called her back.

"What are you afraid of, my dear child? Come and live with me, and if you do the house-work well and orderly, things shall go well with you. You must take great pains to make my bed well, and shake it up thoroughly, so that the feathers fly about, and then in the world it snows, for I am Mother Hulda."*

As the old woman spoke so kindly, the girl took courage, consented, and went to her work. She did everything to the old woman's satisfaction, and shook the bed with such a will that the feathers flew about like snow-

*In Hesse, when it snows, they say, "Mother Hulda is making her bed."

flakes: and so she led a good life, had never a cross word, but boiled and roast meat every day. When she had lived a long time with Mother Hulda, she began to feel sad, not knowing herself what ailed her; at last she began to think she must be home-sick; and although she was a thousand times better off than at home where she was, yet she had a

great longing to go home. At last she said to her mistress, "I am home-sick, and although I am very well off here, I cannot stay any longer; I must go back to my own home."

Mother Hulda answered, "It pleases me well that you should wish to go home, and, as you have served me faithfully, I will undertake to send you there!"

She took her by the hand and led her to a large door standing open, and as she was passing through it there fell upon her a heavy shower of gold, and the gold hung all about her, so that she was covered with it.

"All this is yours, because you have been so industrious," said Mother Hulda; and, besides that, she returned to her her spindle, the very same that she had dropped in the well. And then the door was shut again, and the girl found herself back again in the world, not far from her mother's house; and as she passed through the yard the cock stood on the top of the well and cried,

"Cock-a-doodle doo!
Our golden girl has come home too!"

Then she went in to her mother, and as she had returned covered with gold she was well received.

So the girl related all her history, and what had happened to her, and when the mother heard how she came to have such great riches she began to wish that her ugly and idle daughter might have the same good fortune. So she sent her to sit by the well and spin; and in order to make her spindle bloody she put her hand into the thorn hedge. Then she threw the spindle into the well, and jumped in herself. She found herself, like her sister, in the beautiful meadow, and followed the same path, and when she came to the baker's oven, the bread cried out, "Oh, take me out, take me out, or I shall burn; I am quite done already!"

But the lazy-bones answered, "I have no desire to black my hands," and went on farther. Soon she came to the apple-tree, who called out, "Oh, shake me, shake me, we apples are all of us ripe!"

But she answered, "That is all very fine; suppose one of you should fall on my head," and went on farther. When she came to Mother Hulda's house she did not feel afraid, as she knew beforehand of her great teeth, and entered into her service at once. The first day she put her hand well to the work, and was industrious, and did everything Mother Hulda bade her, because of the gold she expected; but the second day she began to be idle, and the third day still more so, so that she would not get up in the morning. Neither did she make Mother Hulda's bed as it ought to have been made, and did not shake it for the feathers to fly about. So that Mother Hulda soon grew tired of her, and gave her warning, at which the lazy thing was well pleased, and thought that now the shower of gold was coming; so

Mother Hulda led her to the door, and as she stood in the doorway, instead of the shower And the king's daughter became a of gold a great kettle full of pitch was emptied over her.

"That is the reward for your service," said Mother Hulda, and shut the door. So the lazy girl came home all covered with pitch, and the cock on the top of the well seeing her, cried,

"Cock-a-doodle doo!
Our dirty girl has come home too!"

And the pitch remained sticking to her fast, and never, as long as she lived, could it be got off.

here was once a miller who was poor, but he had one beautiful daughter. It happened one day that he came to speak with the king, and, to give himself consequence, he told him that he had a daughter who could spin gold out of straw. The king said to the miller, "That is an art that pleases me well; if thy daughter is as clever as you say, bring her to my castle to-morrow, that I may put her to the proof."

When the girl was brought to him, he led her into a room that was quite full of straw, and gave her a wheel and spindle, and said, "Now set to work, and if by the early morning thou hast not spun this straw to gold thou shalt die." And he shut the door himself, and left her there alone.

And so the poor miller's daughter was left there sitting, and could not think what to do for her life: she had no notion how to set to work to spin gold from straw, and her distress grew so great that she began to weep. Then all at once the door opened, and in came a little man, who said, "Good evening, miller's daughter; why are you crying?"

"Oh!" answered the girl, "I have got to

spin gold out of straw, and I don't understand the business."

Then the little man said, "What will you give me if I spin it for you?"

"My necklace," said the girl.

The little man took the necklace, seated himself before the wheel, and whirr, whirr, whirr! three times round and the bobbin was full; then he took up another, and whirr, whirr, whirr! three times round, and that was full; and so he went on till the morning, when all the straw had been spun, and all the bobbins were full of gold. At sunrise came the king, and when he saw the gold he was astonished and very much rejoiced, for he was very avaricious. He had the miller's daughter taken into another room filled with straw, much bigger than the last, and told her that as she valued her life she must spin it all in one night. The girl did not know what to do, so she began to cry, and then the door opened, and the little man appeared and said, "What will you give me if I spin all this straw into gold?" "The ring from my finger," answered the girl.

So the little man took the ring, and began again to send the wheel whirring round, and by the next morning all the straw was spun into glistening gold. The king was rejoiced beyond measure at the sight, but as he could never have enough of gold, he had the miller's daughter taken into a still larger room full of straw, and said, "This, too, must be spun in one night, and if you accomplish it you shall be my wife." For he thought, "Although she is but a miller's daughter, I am not likely to find any one richer in the whole world."

As soon as the girl was left alone, the little man appeared for the third time and said, "What will you give me if I spin the straw for you this time?"

"I have nothing left to give," answered the girl.

"Then you must promise me the first child you have after you are queen," said the little man.

"But who knows whether that will happen?" thought the girl; but as she did not know what else to do in her necessity, she promised the little man what he desired, upon which he began to spin, until all the straw was gold. And when in the morning the king came and found all done according to his wish, he caused the wedding to be held at once, and the miller's pretty daughter became a queen.

In a year's time she brought a fine child into the world, and thought no more of the little man; but one day he came suddenly into her room, and said, "Now give me what you promised me."

The queen was terrified greatly, and offered the little man all the riches of the kingdom if he would only leave the child; but the little man said, "No, I would rather have something living than all the treasures of the world."

Then the queen began to lament and to weep, so that the little man had pity upon her.

"I will give you three days," said he, "and if at the end of that time you cannot tell my name, you must give up the child to me."

Then the queen spent the whole night in thinking over all the names that she had ever heard, and sent a messenger through the land to ask far and wide for all the names that could be found. And when the little man came next day (beginning with Caspar, Melchior, Balthazar), she repeated all she knew, and went through the whole list, but after each the little man said, "That is not my name."

The second day the queen sent to inquire of all the neighbors what the servants were called, and told the little man all the most unusual and singular names, saying, "Perhaps you are called Roast-ribs, or Sheepshanks, or Spindleshanks?" But he answered nothing but "That is not my name."

The third day the messenger came back again, and said, "I have not been able to find one single new name; but as I passed through the woods I came to a high hill, and near it was a little house, and before the house burned a fire, and round the fire danced a comical little man, and he hopped on one leg and cried,

"To-day do I bake, to-morrow I brew,
The day after that the queen's child comes in;
And oh! I am glad that nobody knew
That the name I am called is Rumpelstiltskin!"

You cannot think how pleased the queen was to hear that name, and soon afterwards, when the little man walked in and said, "Now, Mrs. Queen, what is my name?" she said at first, "Are you called Jack?"

"No," answered he.

"Are you called Harry?" she asked again.

"No," answered he. And then she said, "Then perhaps your name is Rumpel-stiltskin!"

The devil told you that! the devil told you that!" cried the little man, and in his anger he stamped with his right foot so hard that it went into the ground above his knee; then he seized his left foot with both his hands in such a fury that he split in two, and there was an end of him.

There was once a poor countryman who used to sit in the chimney corner all evening and poke the fire, while his wife sat at her spinning-wheel.

And he used to say, "How dull it is without any children about us; our house is so quiet, and other people's houses so noisy and merry!"

"Yes," answered his wife, and sighed, "if we could only have one, and that one ever so little, no bigger than my thumb, how happy I should be! It would, indeed, be having our heart's desire."

Now, it happened that after a while the woman had a child who was perfect in all his limbs, but no bigger than a thumb. Then the parents said, "He is just what we wished for, and we will love him very much," and they named him according to his stature, "Tom Thumb." And though they gave him plenty of nourishment, he grew no bigger, but remained exactly the same size as when he was first born; and he had very good faculties, and was very quick and prudent, so that all he did prospered.

One day his father made ready to go into the forest to cut wood, and he said, as if to himself, "Now, I wish there was some one to bring the cart to meet me."

"O father," cried Tom Thumb, "I can bring the cart, let me alone for that, and in proper time, too!"

Then the father laughed, and said, "How will you manage that? You are much too little to hold the reins."

"That has nothing to do with it, father; while my mother goes on with her spinning I will sit in the horse's ear and tell him where to go."

"Well," answered the father, "we will try it for once."

When it was time to set off, the mother went on spinning, after setting Tom Thumb in the horse's ear; and so he drove off crying "Gee-up, gee-wo!"

So the horse went on quite as if his master were driving him, and drew the wagon along the right road to the wood.

Now it happened just as they turned a corner, and the little fellow was calling out "Gee-up!" that two strange men passed by.

"Look," said one of them, "how is this? There goes a wagon, and the driver is calling to the horse, and yet he is nowhere to be seen."

"It is very strange," said the other; "we will follow the wagon, and see where it belongs."

And the wagon went right through the wood, up to the place where the wood had been hewed. When Tom Thumb caught sight of his father, he cried out, "Look, father, here am I with the wagon; now, take me down."

The father held the horse with his left hand, and with the right he lifted down his little son out of the horse's ear, and Tom Thumb sat down on a stump, quite happy and content. When the two strangers saw him they were struck dumb with wonder. At last one of them, taking the other aside, said to him, "Look here, the little chap would make our fortune if we were to show him in the town for money. Suppose we buy him."

So they went up to the woodcutter, and said, "Sell the little man to us; we will take care he shall come to no harm."

"No," answered the father; "he is the apple of my eye, and not for all the money in the world would I sell him."

But Tom Thumb, when he heard what was going on, climbed up by his father's coat tails, and, perching himself on his shoulder, he whispered in his ear, "Father, you might as well let me go. I will soon come back again."

Then the father gave him up to the two men for a large piece of money. They asked him where he would like to sit.

"Oh, put me on the brim of your hat," said he. "There I can walk about and view the country, and be in no danger of falling off."

So they did as he wished, and when Tom Thumb had taken leave of his father, they set off all together. And they travelled on until it grew dusk, and the little fellow asked to be set down a little while for a change, and after some difficulty they consented. So the man took him down from his hat, and set him in a field by the roadside, and he ran away directly, and, after creeping about among the furrows, he slipped suddenly into a mouse-hole, just what he was looking for.

"Good evening, my masters, you can go home without me!" cried he to them, laughing. They ran up and felt about with their sticks in the mouse-hole, but in vain. Tom Thumb crept farther and farther in, and as it was growing dark, they had to make the best of their way home, full of vexation, and with empty purses.

When Tom Thumb found they were gone, he crept out of his hiding place underground.

"It is dangerous work groping about these holes in the darkness," said he; "I might easily break my neck."

But by good fortune he came upon an empty snail shell.

"That's all right," said he. "Now I can get safely through the night;" and he settled himself down in it. Before he had time to get to sleep, he heard two men pass by, and one was saying to the other, "How can we man-

age to get hold of the rich parson's gold and silver?"

"I can tell you how," cried Tom Thumb.

"How is this?" said one of the thieves, quite frightened, "I hear some one speak!"

So they stood still and listened, and Tom Thumb spoke again.

"Take me with you; I will show you how to do it!"

"Where are you, then?" asked they.

"Look about on the ground and notice where the voice comes from," answered he.

At last they found him, and lifted him up.

"You little elf," said they, "how can you help us?"

"Look here," answered he, "I can easily creep between the iron bars of the parson's room and hand out to you whatever you would like to have."

"Very well," said they, "we will try what you can do."

So when they came to the parsonage-house, Tom Thumb crept into the room, but cried out with all his might, "Will you have all that is here?" So the thieves were terrified, and said, "Do speak more softly, lest any one should be awaked."

But Tom Thumb made as if he did not hear them, and cried out again, "What would you like? will you have all that is here?" so that the cook, who was sleeping in a room hard by, heard it, and raised herself in bed and listened. The thieves, however, in their fear of being discovered, had run back part of the way, but they took courage again, thinking that it was only a jest of the little fellow's. So they came back and whispered to him to be serious, and to hand them out something.

Then Tom Thumb called out once more as loud as he could, "Oh yes, I will give it all to you, only put out your hands."

Then the listening maid heard him distinctly that time, and jumped out of bed, and burst open the door. The thieves ran off as if the wild huntsman were behind them; but the maid, as she could see nothing, went to fetch a light. And when she came back with one, Tom Thumb had taken himself off, without being seen by her, into the barn; and the maid, when she had looked in every hole and corner and found nothing, went back to bed at last, and thought that she must have been dreaming with her eyes and ears open.

So Tom Thumb crept among the hay, and

found a comfortable nook to sleep in, where he intended to remain until it was day, and then to go home to his father and mother. But other things were to befall him; indeed, there is nothing but trouble and worry in this world! The maid got up at dawn of day to feed the cows. The first place she went to was the barn, where she took up an armful of hay, and it happened to be the very heap in which Tom Thumb lay asleep. And he was so fast asleep, that he was aware of nothing, and never woke until he was in the mouth of the cow, who had taken him up with the hay.

"Oh dear," cried he, "how is it that I have got into a mill!" but he soon found out where he was, and he had to be very careful not to get between the cow's teeth, and at last he had to descend into the cow's stomach.

"The windows were forgotten when this little room was built," said he, "and the sunshine cannot get in; there is no light to be had."

His quarters were in every way unpleasant to him, and, what was the worst, new hay was constantly coming in, and the space was being filled up. At last he cried out in his extremity, as loud as he could.

"No more hay for me! no more hay for me!"

The maid was then milking the cow, and as she heard a voice, but could see no one, and as it was the same voice that she had heard in the night, she was so frightened that she fell off her stool, and spilt the milk. Then she ran in great haste to her master, crying, "Oh, master dear, the cow spoke!"

"You must be crazy," answered her master, and he went himself to the cow-house to see what was the matter. No sooner had he put his foot inside the door, than Tom Thumb cried out again, "No more hay for me! no more hay for me!"

Then the parson himself was frightened, supposing that a bad spirit had entered into the cow, and he ordered her to be put to death. So she was killed, but the stomach, where Tom Thumb was lying, was thrown upon a dunghill. Tom Thumb had great trouble to work his way out of it, and he had just made a space big enough for his head to go through, when a new misfortune happened. A hungry wolf ran up and swallowed the whole stomach at one gulp. But Tom Thumb did not lose courage. "Perhaps," thought he, "the wolf will listen to reason," and he cried out from the inside of the wolf, "My dear wolf, I can tell you where to get a splendid meal!"

"Where is it to be had?" asked the wolf.

"In such and such a house, and you must creep into it through the drain, and there you will find cakes and bacon and broth, as much as you can eat," and he described to him his father's house. The wolf needed not to be told twice. He squeezed himself through the drain in the night, and feasted in the store-room to his heart's content. When, at last, he was satisfied, he wanted to go away again, but he had become so big, that to creep the same way back was impossible. This Tom Thumb had reckoned upon, and began to make a terrible din inside the wolf, crying and calling as loud as he could.

"Will you be quiet?" said the wolf; "you will wake the folks up!"

"Look here," cried the little man, "you are very well satisfied, and now I will do something for my own enjoyment," and began again to make all the noise he could. At last the father and mother were awakened, and they ran to the room-door and peeped through the chink, and when they saw a wolf in occupation, they ran and fetched weapons—the man an axe, and the wife a scythe.

"Stay behind," said the man, as they entered the room; "when I have given him a blow, and it does not seem to have killed him, then you must cut at him with your scythe."

Then Tom Thumb heard his father's voice, and cried, "Dear father, I am here in the wolf's inside."

Then the father called out full of joy, "Thank heaven that we have found our dear child!" and told his wife to keep the scythe out of the way, lest Tom Thumb should be hurt with it. Then he drew near and struck the wolf such a blow on the head that he fell down dead; and then he fetched a knife and a pair of scissors, slit up the wolf's body, and let out the little fellow.

"Oh, what anxiety we have felt about you!" said the father.

"Yes, father, I have seen a good deal of the world, and I am very glad to breathe fresh air again."

"And where have you been all this time?" asked his father.

"Oh, I have been in a mouse-hole and a snail's shell, in a cow's stomach and a wolf's inside: now, I think, I will stay at home."

"And we will not part with you for all the kingdoms of the world," cried the parents, as they kissed and hugged their dear little Tom Thumb. And they gave him something to eat and drink, and a new suit of clothes, as his old ones were soiled with travel.

here was once a king who was sick, and no one thought he would live. His three sons were very sad. They went down into the palace garden and wept, and there they met an old man, who asked them what the trouble was. They told him their father was very sick and would surely die, for nothing seemed to do him any good. The old man said: "I know of a remedy: the Water of Life. If he drinks of it, he will get well, but it's hard to find." "I'll find it," said the eldest, and he went to the sick king and asked him for leave to search for the Water of Life, since that alone could cure him. "No," said the king, "the danger is too great. I would rather die." But the son begged and pleaded until the king finally consented. The prince thought in his heart: "If I bring him the Water of Life, my father will love me the best, and I shall inherit the kingdom."

So he started out and when he had ridden awhile, a dwarf, who was standing on the road, called out to him: "Where are you going so fast?" "You stupid runt," said the prince haughtily, "what business is it of

The dwarf was furious and cursed him. (page 145)

yours?" And he rode on. The dwarf was furious and cursed him. The prince soon came to a ravine. The farther he rode the closer the mountains came together, and in the end the path was so narrow that his horse couldn't take another step. The prince could neither turn his horse around nor dismount, and all he could do was sit there, wedged tight in his saddle. The sick king waited in vain for his eldest son to return, and then one day the second son said: "Father, let me go and look for the Water." He thought to himself: "If my brother is dead, the kingdom will fall to me." At first the king didn't want to let him go, but in the end he gave in. So the prince set out, taking the same road as his brother, and he too met the dwarf, who stopped him and asked where he was going so fast. "You little runt," said the prince, "What business is it of yours?" And he rode on without so much as looking around. Whereupon the dwarf cursed him, and like his brother he rode deep into a ravine until he got wedged in and was unable to go forward or backward. That's what happens to haughty people.

When the second son also failed to return, the youngest son asked leave to search for the Water, and the king finally had to let him go. When he met the dwarf and the dwarf asked him where he was going in such a hurry, he stopped and answered him: "I'm looking for the Water of Life, because my father is deathly sick." "Do you know where to find it?" "No," said the prince. "Since you've spoken kindly and haven't been haughty like your two wicked brothers, I'll tell you where the Water of Life is and how to get there. It springs from a fountain in the courtyard of an enchanted castle, but you'll never get in unless I give you an iron wand and two loaves of bread. Strike the castle gate three times with the wand and it will open. Inside, there will be two lions with gaping jaws, but if you throw a loaf to each of them, they will calm down. Then you must hurry and take the Water of Life before the clock strikes twelve, because otherwise the gate will close and you will be locked in." The prince thanked him, took the wand and the bread, and went his way. When he reached the castle, everything was just as the dwarf had said. The gate opened at the third stroke of the wand, and when he had calmed the lions with the bread, he went into the castle and came to a big, beautiful hall, full of enchanted princes. He drew the rings from their fingers and also took a sword and a loaf of bread that he found in the great hall. Farther on he came to a room, where a beautiful maiden was standing. She was overjoyed to see him, kissed him and told him he had set her free. "My whole kingdom will be yours," she said. "If you come back in a year's time we shall celebrate our wedding." Then she told him where to find the fountain with the Water of Life and bade him hurry and draw the water before the clock struck twelve. He went on and came at last to a room with a beautiful, freshly made bed in it. As he was tired, he thought he would rest awhile. He lay down and fell asleep, and when he awoke the clock was striking a quarter to twelve. He jumped up in a fright, ran to the fountain, drew the water in a cup that he found nearby, and hurried away. Just as he was passing through the iron gate, the clock struck twelve, and the gate slammed with such force that it took off a piece of his heel.

All the same, he was glad to have found the Water of Life, and started home. On the way he came to the dwarf and when the dwarf saw the sword and the loaf, he said: "Those are great treasures you've come by. With that sword you can defeat whole armies, and that loaf will always be the same size no matter how much is eaten from it." But the prince didn't want to go home to his father without his brothers, and he said: "Dear dwarf, could you tell me where my two brothers are? They set out in search of the Water of Life before I did, and they never came back." "They're wedged in between mountains," said the dwarf. "I wished them there because they were haughty." The prince pleaded and at length the dwarf released them, though he warned him, saying: "Don't trust them. They have wicked hearts."

When his brothers appeared, he was glad

to see them. He told them of his adventures, how he had found the Water of Life and brought back a cupful of it, and how he had saved a beautiful princess, who was going to wait a year for him and then they were going to be married and he would be king over a great kingdom. The brothers rode on together and came to a country where war and famine were raging and the misery was so great that the king of the country thought he would perish. The prince went to the king and gave him the loaf, whereupon the king fed all his people, and stilled their hunger. Next the prince gave the king his sword, the king destroyed the enemy armies, and after that he was able to live in peace. Then the prince took back his loaf and his sword, and the three brothers rode on. They passed through two more countries where war and famine were raging, and in both the prince lent the kings his loaf and his sword, so, all in all, he saved three kingdoms. Then they boarded a ship and sailed across the sea. During the voyage the two elder brothers went aside and said: "Our young brother has found the Water of Life and we haven't found anything. Our father will reward him by giving him the kingdom, which should properly be ours, and he will rob us of our birthright." They longed for revenge and decided on a way to destroy him. They waited until he was fast asleep, and then they poured the Water of Life out of his cup, took it away, and filled the cup with bitter sea water.

When they got home, the youngest brother brought the sick king his cup, expecting him to drink and be cured. But the king had barely tasted the bitter sea water when he became sicker than ever. As he was lamenting, his two elder sons came in and accused the youngest of wanting to poison him. Then they brought in the real Water of Life and handed it to him. The moment he drank of it he felt his sickness leaving him, and was as strong and healthy as in the days of his youth. The two deceivers went to the youngest brother and jeered at him: "Oh yes," they said, "you found the Water of Life, but much good it has done you. Yours the hardship and ours the reward. You should have been smarter and kept your eyes open. We took it away from you on the ship, while you were sleeping, and a year from now one of us will go and claim the beautiful princess. But whatever you do, don't tell our father about this. He wouldn't believe you, and if you say so much as a single word you will die, but if you keep silent your life will be spared."

The old king was very angry, for he thought his youngest had wanted to kill him. He summoned his council and had them sentence the boy to be secretly shot. One day the prince, who suspected no evil, went hunting, and the king's huntsman rode along with him. When they were all alone in the forest, the huntsman looked so sad that the prince asked him: "Dear huntsman, what's the matter?" "I can't tell you," said the huntsman, "and yet I should." "Speak up," said the prince. "Whatever it is, I'll forgive you." "Well," said the huntsman, "I'm supposed to kill you. The king ordered me to." The prince was aghast. "Dear huntsman," he said, "let me live! I'll give you my royal garments. Give me your lowly ones in exchange." "Gladly," said the hunter. "I wouldn't have been able to shoot you in any case." Whereupon they changed clothes. Then the huntsman went home and the prince went deeper into the forest.

Some time later three wagonloads of gold and precious stones came to the king for his youngest son. They had been sent in token of gratitude by the three kings who had destroyed their enemies with the prince's sword and fed their people with his loaf. The old king thought to himself: "Can my son have been innocent?" And he said aloud: "If only he were alive! I can't forgive myself for having him killed." At that the huntsman spoke up: "He is alive. I couldn't bring myself to carry out your order." And then he told the king what had happened. A weight fell from the king's heart and he had it proclaimed in all the kingdoms that his son was free to come home and would be welcomed with open arms.

Meanwhile the princess had a golden road built leading to her castle, and said to her guards: "The man who comes riding straight up to me in the middle of the road will be the right one and you must let him in. If anyone rides alongside the road, he will not be the right man, and you are not to let him in." When the year had almost passed, the eldest son thought he would hurry to the princess and pass himself off as her savior. He fully expected to win her as his wife and become master over her kingdom as well. He started out, and when he came to the castle and saw the beautiful golden road, he thought: "It would be a pity to ride on such a beautiful road." So he veered off and went on to the right of it. When he reached the gate, the guards said to him: "You are not the right man. Go away." A little later the second prince started out, and when he came to the golden road and his horse had only set one foot on it, he thought: "It would be a pity. What if the hoofbeats should crack it!" So he veered off and went on to the left of the road. When he reached the gate, the guards said: "You are not the right man. Go away." When the year had wholly passed, the third prince decided to leave his forest, ride away to his beloved, and forget his sorrows with her. Throughout his journey he thought of her and wished he were already with her, so when he got to the golden road he didn't even see it. His horse galloped right up the middle of it, and when he reached the gate it was opened. The princess welcomed him joyfully and said: "You are my savior and the lord of my kingdom." The marriage was celebrated with great rejoicing, and when it was over she told him that his father had sent for him and had forgiven him. Thereupon he rode home and told his father how his brothers had cheated him and how he had kept silent. The king wanted to punish them, but they had boarded a ship and sailed away, and they never came back as long as they lived.

ear a great forest there lived a poor woodcutter and his wife, and his two children; the boy's name was Hansel and the girl's Grethel. They had very little to bite or to sup, and once, when there was great dearth in the land, the man could not even gain the daily bread. As he lay in bed one night thinking of this, and turning and tossing, he sighed heavily, and said to his wife, "What will become of us? we cannot even feed our children; there is nothing left for ourselves."

"I will tell you what, husband," answered the wife; "we will take the children early in the morning into the forest, where it is thickest; we will make them a fire, and we will give each of them a piece of bread, then we will go to our work and leave them alone; they will never find the way home again, and we shall be quit of them."

"No, wife," said the man, "I cannot do that; I cannot find in my heart to take my children into the forest and to leave them there alone; the wild animals would soon come and devour them."

"O you fool," said she, "then we will all four starve; you had better get the coffins ready,"—and she left him no peace until he consented.

"But I really pity the poor children," said the man.

The two children had not been able to sleep for hunger, and had heard what their step-mother had said to their father. Grethel wept bitterly, and said to Hansel, "It is all over with us."

"Do be quiet, Grethel," said Hansel, "and do not fret; I will manage something." And when the parents had gone to sleep he got up, put on his little coat, opened the back door, and slipped out. The moon was shining brightly, and the white flints that lay in front of the house glistened like pieces of silver. Hansel stooped and filled the little pocket of his coat as full as it would hold. Then he went back again, and said to Grethel, "Be easy, little sister, and go to sleep quietly; God will not forsake us," and laid himself down again in his bed.

When the day was breaking, and before the sun had risen, the wife came and awakened the two children, saying, "Get up, you lazy bones; we are going into the forest to cut wood."

Then she gave each of them a piece of bread, and said, "That is for dinner, and you must not eat it before then, for you will get no more."

Grethel carried the bread under her apron, for Hansel had his pockets full of the flints. Then they set off all together on their way to the forest. When they had gone a little way Hansel stood still and looked back towards the house, and this he did again and again, till his father said to him, "Hansel, what are you looking at? take care not to forget your legs."

"O father," said Hansel, "I am looking at my little white kitten, who is sitting up on the roof to bid me good-bye."

"You young fool," said the woman, "that is not your kitten, but the sunshine on the chimney-pot."

Of course Hansel had not been looking at his kitten, but had been taking every now and then a flint from his pocket and dropping it on the road.

When they reached the middle of the forest the father told the children to collect wood to make a fire to keep them warm; and Hansel and Grethel gathered brushwood enough for a little mountain; and it was set on fire, and when the flame was burning quite high the wife said, "Now lie down by the fire and rest yourselves, you children, and we will go and cut wood; and when we are ready we will come and fetch you."

So Hansel and Grethel sat by the fire, and at noon they each ate their pieces of bread. They thought their father was in the wood all the time, as they seemed to hear the strokes of the axe: but really it was only a dry branch hanging to a withered tree that the wind moved to and fro. So when they had stayed there a long time their eyelids closed with weariness, and they fell fast asleep. When at last they woke it was night, and Grethel began to cry, and said, "How shall we ever get out of this wood?" But Hansel comforted her, saying, "Wait a little while longer, until the moon rises, and then we can easily find the way home."

And when the full moon got up Hansel took his little sister by the hand, and followed the way where the flint stones shone like silver, and showed them the road. They walked on the whole night through, and at the break of day they came to their father's house. They knocked at the door, and when the wife opened it and saw that it was Hansel and Grethel she said, "You naughty children, why did you sleep so long in the wood? we thought you were never coming home again!"

But the father was glad, for it had gone to his heart to leave them both in the woods alone.

Not very long after that there was again great scarcity in those parts, and the children heard their mother say at night in bed to their father, "Everything is finished up; we have only half a loaf, and after that the tale comes to an end. The children must be off; we will take them farther into the wood this time, so that they shall not be able to find the way back again; there is no other way to manage."

The man felt sad at heart, and he thought, "It would be better to share one's last morsel with one's children."

But the wife would listen to nothing that he said, but scolded and reproached him. He who says A must say B too, and when a man has given in once he has to do it a second time.

But the children were not asleep, and had heard all the talk. When the parents had gone to sleep Hansel got up to go out and get more flint stones, as he did before, but the wife had locked the door, and Hansel could not get out; but he comforted his little sister, and said, "Don't cry, Grethel, and go to sleep quietly, and God will help us."

Early the next morning the wife came and pulled the children out of bed. She gave them each a little piece of bread—less than before; and on the way to the wood Hansel crumbled the bread in his pocket, and often stopped to throw a crumb on the ground.

"Hansel, what are you stopping behind and staring for?" said the father.

"I am looking at my little pigeon sitting on the roof, to say good-bye to me," answered Hansel.

"You fool," said the wife, "that is no pigeon, but the morning sun shining on the chimney-pots."

Hansel went on as before, and strewed bread crumbs all along the road.

The woman led the children far into the wood, where they had never been before in all their lives. And again there was a large fire made, and the mother said, "Sit still there, you children, and when you are tired you can go to sleep; we are going into the forest to cut wood, and in the evening, when we are ready to go home we will come and fetch you."

So when noon came Grethel shared her bread with Hansel, who had strewed his along the road. Then they went to sleep, and the evening passed, and no one came for the poor children. When they awoke it was dark night, and Hansel comforted his little sister, and said, "Wait a little, Grethel, until the moon gets up, then we shall be able to see the way home by the crumbs of bread that I have scattered along it."

So when the moon rose they got up, but they could find no crumbs of bread, for the birds of the woods and of the fields had come and picked them up. Hansel thought they might find the way all the same, but they could not. They went on all that night, and the next day from the morning until the evening, but they could not find the way out of the wood, and they were very hungry, for they had nothing to eat but the few berries they could pick up. And when they were so tired that they could no longer drag themselves along, they lay down under a tree and fell asleep.

It was now the third morning since they had left their father's house. They were always trying to get back to it, but instead of that they only found themselves farther in the wood, and if help had not soon come they would have been starved. About noon they saw a pretty snow-white bird sitting on a bough, and singing so sweetly that they stopped to listen. And when he had finished the bird spread his wings and flew before them, and they followed after him until they came to a little house, and the bird perched on the roof, and when they came nearer they saw that the house was built of bread, and roofed with cakes; and the window was of transparent sugar.

"We will have some of this," said Hansel, "and make a fine meal. I will eat a piece of the roof, Grethel, and you can have some of the window—that will taste sweet."

So Hansel reached up and broke off a bit of the roof, just to see how it tasted, and Grethel stood by the window and gnawed at it. Then they heard a thin voice call out from inside,

> "Nibble, nibble, like a mouse,
> Who is nibbling at my house?"

And the children answered,

> "Never mind,
> It is the wind."

And they went on eating, never disturbing _____

themselves. Hansel, who found that the roof tasted very nice, took down a great piece of it, and Grethel pulled out a large round window-pane, and sat her down and began upon it. Then the door opened, and an aged woman came out leaning upon a crutch. Hansel and Grethel felt very frightened, and let fall what they had in their hands. The old woman, however, nodded her head, and said, "Ah, my dear children, how come you here? you must come indoors and stay with me, you will be no trouble."

So she took them each by the hand, and led them into her little house. And there they found a good meal laid out, of milk and pancakes, with sugar, apples, and nuts. After that she showed them two little white beds, and Hansel and Grethel laid themselves down on them, and thought they were in heaven.

The old woman, although her behavior was so kind, was a wicked witch, who lay in wait for children, and had built the little house on purpose to entice them. When they were once inside she used to kill them, cook them, and eat them, and then it was a feast-day with her. The witch's eyes were red, and she could not see very far, but she had a keen scent, like the beasts, and knew very well when human creatures were near. When she knew that Hansel and Grethel were coming, she gave a spiteful laugh, and said triumphantly, "I have them, and they shall not escape me!"

Early in the morning, before the children were awake, she got up to look at them, and as they lay sleeping so peacefully with round rosy cheeks, she said to herself, "What a fine feast I shall have!"

Then she grasped Hansel with her withered hand, and led him into a little stable, and shut him up behind a grating; and call and scream as he might, it was no good. Then she went back to Grethel and shook her, crying, "Get up, lazy bones; fetch water, and cook something nice for your brother; he is outside in the stable, and must be fattened up. And when he is fat enough I will eat him."

Grethel began to weep bitterly, but it was of no use, she had to do what the wicked witch bade her.

And so the best kind of victuals was cooked for poor Hansel, while Grethel got nothing but crab-shells. Each morning the old woman visited the little stable, and cried, "Hansel, stretch out your finger, that I may tell if you will soon be fat enough."

Hansel, however, used to hold out a little bone, and the old woman, who had weak eyes, could not see what it was, and supposing it to be Hansel's finger, wondered very much that it was not getting fatter. When four weeks had passed and Hansel seemed to remain so thin, she lost patience and could wait no longer.

"Now then, Grethel," cried she to the little girl; "be quick and draw water; be Hansel fat or be he lean, to-morrow I must kill and cook him."

Oh what a grief for the poor little sister to have to fetch water, and how the tears flowed down over her cheeks!

"Dear God, pray help us!" cried she; "if we had been devoured by wild beasts in the

wood at least we should have died together."

"Spare me your lamentations," said the old woman; "they are of no avail."

Early next morning Grethel had to get up, make the fire, and fill the kettle.

"First we will do the baking," said the old woman; "I have heated the oven already, and kneaded the dough."

She pushed poor Grethel towards the oven, out of which the flames were already shining.

"Creep in," said the witch, "and see if it is properly hot, so that the bread may be baked."

And Grethel once in, she meant to shut the door upon her and let her be baked, and then she would have eaten her. But Grethel perceived her intention, and said, "I don't know how to do it: how shall I get in?"

"Stupid goose," said the old woman, "the opening is big enough, do you see? I could get in myself!" and she stooped down and put her head in the oven's mouth. Then Grethel gave her a push, so that she went in farther, and she shut the iron door upon her, and put up the bar. Oh how frightfully she howled! but Grethel ran away, and left the wicked witch to burn miserably. Grethel went straight to Hansel, opened the stable-door, and cried, "Hansel, we are free! the old witch is dead!"

Then out flew Hansel like a bird from its cage as soon as the door is opened. How rejoiced they both were! how they fell each on the other's neck! and danced about, and kissed each other! And as they had nothing more to fear they went over all the old witch's house, and in every corner there stood chests of pearls and precious stones.

"This is something better than flint stones," said Hansel, as he filled his pockets, and Grethel, thinking she also would like to carry something home with her, filled her apron full.

"Now, away we go," said Hansel;—"if we only can get out of the witch's wood."

When they had journeyed a few hours they came to a great piece of water.

"We can never get across this," said Hansel, "I see no stepping-stones and no bridge."

"And there is no boat either," said Grethel; "but here comes a white duck; if I ask her she will help us over." So she cried,

"Duck, duck, here we stand,
Hansel and Grethel, on the land,
Stepping-stones and bridge we lack,
Carry us over on your nice white back."

And the duck came accordingly, and Hansel got upon her and told his sister to come too.

"No," answered Grethel, "that would be too hard upon the duck; we can go separately, one after the other."

And that was how it was managed, and after that they went on happily, until they came to the wood, and the way grew more and more familiar, till at last they saw in the distance their father's house. Then they ran till they came up to it, rushed in at the door, and fell on their father's neck. The man had not had a quiet hour since he left his children in the wood; but the wife was dead. And when Grethel opened her apron the pearls and precious stones were scattered all over the room, and Hansel took one handful after another out of his pocket. Then was all care at an end, and they lived in great joy together.

> Sing every one,
> My story is done,
> And look! round the house
> There runs a little mouse,
> He that can catch her before she scampers in,
> May make himself a very very large
> fur-cap out of her skin

here was a king who had twelve beautiful daughters. They slept in twelve beds all in one room; and when they went to bed, the doors were shut and locked up; but every morning their shoes were found to be quite worn through as if they had been danced in all night; and yet nobody could find out how it happened, or where they had been.

Then the king made it known to all the land, that if any person could discover the secret, and find out where it was that the princesses danced in the night, he should have the one he liked best for his wife, and should be king after his death; but whoever tried and did not succeed, after three days and nights, should be put to death.

A king's son soon came. He was well entertained, and in the evening was taken to the chamber next to the one where the princesses lay in their twelve beds. There he was to sit and watch where they went to dance; and, in order that nothing might pass without his hearing it, the door of his chamber was left open. But the king's son soon fell asleep; and when he awoke in the morning he found that the princesses had all been dancing, for the soles of their shoes were full of holes. The same thing happened the second and third night: so the king ordered his head to be cut off. After him came several others; but they had all the same luck, and all lost their lives in the same manner.

Now it chanced that an old soldier, who had been wounded in battle and could fight no longer, passed through the country where this king reigned: and as he was traveling through a wood, he met an old woman, who asked him where he was going. "I hardly know where I am going, or what I had better do," said the soldier; "but I think I should like very well to find out where it is that the princesses dance, and then in time I might be a king," "Well," said the old dame, "that is no very hard task: only take care not to drink any of the wine which one of the princesses will bring to you in the evening; and as soon as she leaves you, pretend to be fast asleep."

Then she gave him a cloak, and said, "As soon as you put that on you will become invisible, and you will then be able to follow the princesses wherever they go." When the soldier heard all this good counsel, he determined to try his luck: so he went to the king, and said he was willing to undertake the task.

He was as well received as the others had been, and the king ordered fine royal robes to be given him; and when the evening came he was led to the outer chamber. Just as he was going to lie down, the eldest of the princesses brought him a cup of wine; but the soldier threw it all away secretly, taking care not to drink a drop. Then he laid himself down on his bed, and in a little while began to snore very loud as if he was fast asleep. When the twelve princesses heard this they laughed heartily: and the eldest said, "This fellow too might have done a wiser thing than lose his life in this way!" Then they rose up and opened their drawers and boxes, and took out all their fine clothes, and dressed themselves at the glass, and skipped about as if they were eager to begin dancing. But the youngest said, "I don't know how it is, while you are so happy I feel very uneasy; I am sure some mischance will befall us." "You simpleton," said the eldest, "you are always afraid; have you forgotten how many kings' sons have already watched us in vain? And as for this soldier, even if I had not given him his sleeping draught, he would have slept soundly enough."

When they were all ready, they went and looked at the soldier; but he snored on, and did not stir hand or foot: so they thought they were quite safe; and the eldest went up to her own bed and clapped her hands, and the bed sunk into the floor and a trap-door flew open. The soldier saw them going down

. . . and the soldier, who was all the time invisible, . . . (page 170)

through the trap-door one after another, the eldest leading the way; and thinking he had no time to lose, he jumped up, put on the cloak which the old woman had given him, and followed them; but in the middle of the stairs he trod on the gown of the youngest princess, and she cried out to her sisters, "All is not right; some one took hold of my gown." "You silly creature!" said the eldest, "it is nothing but a nail in the wall." Then down they all went, and at the bottom they found themselves in a most delightful grove of trees; and the leaves were all of silver, and glittered and sparkled beautifully. The soldier wished to take away some token of the place; so he broke off a little branch, and there came a loud noise from the tree. Then the youngest daughter said again, "I am sure all is not right—did not you hear that noise? That never happened before." But the eldest said, "It is only our princes, who are shouting for joy at our approach."

Then they came to another grove of trees, where all the leaves were of gold; and afterwards to a third, where the leaves were all glittering diamonds. And the soldier broke a branch from each; and every time there was a loud noise, which made the youngest sister tremble with fear; but the eldest still said, It was only the princes, who were crying for joy. So they went on till they came to a great lake; and at the side of the lake there lay twelve little boats with twelve handsome princes in them, who seemed to be waiting there for the princesses.

One of the princesses went into each boat, and the soldier stepped into the same boat with the youngest. As they were rowing over the lake, the prince who was in the boat with the youngest princess and the soldier said, "I do not know why it is, but though I am rowing with all my might we do not get on so fast as usual, and I am quite tired: the boat seems very heavy to-day." "It is only the heat of the weather," said the princess; "I feel it very warm too."

On the other side of the lake stood a fine illuminated castle, from which came the merry music of horns and trumpets. There they all landed, and went into the castle, and each prince danced with his princess; and the soldier, who was all the time invisible, danced with them too; and when any of the princesses had a cup of wine set by her, he drank it all up, so that when she put the cup to her mouth it was empty. At this, too, the youngest sister was terribly frightened, but the eldest always silenced her. They danced on till three o'clock in the morning, and then all their shoes were worn out, so that they were obliged to leave off. The princes rowed them back again over the lake (but this time the soldier placed himself in the boat with the eldest princess); and on the opposite shore they took leave of each other, the princesses promising to come again the next night.

When they came to the stairs, the soldier ran on before the princesses, and laid himself down; and as the twelve sisters slowly came up very much tired, they heard him snoring in his bed; so they said, "Now all is quite safe," then they undressed themselves, put away their fine clothes, pulled off their shoes, and went to bed. In the morning the soldier said nothing about what had happened, but determined to see more of this strange adventure, and went again the second and third night; and every thing happened just as before; the princesses danced each time till their shoes were worn to pieces, and then returned home. However, on the third night the soldier carried away one of the golden cups as a token of where he had been.

As soon as the time came when he was to declare the secret, he was taken before the king with the three branches and the golden cup; and the twelve princesses stood listening behind the door to hear what he would say. And when the king asked him, "Where do my twelve daughters dance at night?" he answered, "With twelve princes in a castle underground." And then he told the king all that had happened, and showed him the three branches and the golden cup which he had brought with him. Then the king called for the princesses, and asked them whether what the soldier said was true: and when they saw that they were discovered, and that it was of no use to deny what had happened, they confessed it all. And the king asked the soldier which of them he would choose for his wife; and he answered, "I am not very young, so I will have the eldest."—And they were married that very day, and the soldier was chosen to be the king's heir.

Once on a time a king was hunting in a great wood, and he pursued a wild animal so eagerly that none of his people could follow him. When evening came he stood still, and looking round him he found that he had lost his way; and seeking a path, he found none. Then all at once he saw an old woman with a nodding head coming up to him; and it was a witch.

"My good woman," said he, "can you show me the way out of the wood?"

"Oh yes, my lord king," answered she, "certainly I can; but I must make a condition, and if you do not fulfil it, you will never get out of the wood again, but die there of hunger."

"What is the condition?" asked the king.

"I have a daughter," said the old woman, "who is as fair as any in the world, and if you will take her for your bride, and make her queen, I will show you the way out of the wood."

The king consented, because of the difficulty he was in, and the old woman led him into her little house, and there her daughter was sitting by the fire.

She received the king just as if she had been expecting him, and though he saw that she was very beautiful, she did not please him, and he could not look at her without an inward shudder. Nevertheless, he took the maiden before him on his horse, and the old woman showed him the way, and soon he was in his royal castle again, where the wedding was held.

The king had been married before, and his first wife had left seven children, six boys and one girl, whom he loved better than all the world, and as he was afraid the stepmother might not behave well to them, and perhaps would do them some mischief, he took them to a lonely castle standing in the middle of a wood. There they remained hidden, for the road to it was so hard to find that the king himself could not have found it, had it not been for a clew of yarn, possessing wonderful properties, that a wise woman had given him; when he threw it down before him, it unrolled itself and showed him the way. And the king went so often to see his dear children, that the queen was displeased at his absence; and she became curious and wanted to know what he went out into the wood for so often alone. She bribed his servants with much money, and they showed her the secret, and told her of the clew of yarn, which alone could point the way; then she gave herself no rest until she had found out where the king kept the clew, and then she made some little white silk shirts, and sewed a charm in each, as she had learned witchcraft of her mother. And once when the king had ridden to the hunt, she took the little shirts and went into the wood, and the clew of yarn showed her the way. The children seeing some one in the distance, thought it was their dear father coming to see them, and came jumping for joy to meet him. Then the wicked queen threw over each one of the little shirts, and as soon as the shirts touched their bodies, they were changed into swans, and flew away through the wood. So the queen went home very pleased to think she had got rid of her step-children; but the maiden had not run out with her brothers, and so the queen knew nothing about her. The next day the king went to see his children, but he found nobody but his daughter.

"Where are thy brothers?" asked the king.

"Ah, dear father," answered she, "they are gone away and have left me behind," and then she told him how she had seen from her window her brothers in the guise of swans fly away through the wood, and she showed him the feathers which they had let fall in the courtyard, and which she had picked up. The king was grieved, but he never dreamt that it was the queen who had done this wicked deed, and as he feared lest the maiden also should be stolen away from him, he wished to take her away with him. But she was afraid of the step-mother, and begged the king to let her remain one more night in the castle in the wood.

Then she said to herself, "I must stay here no longer, but go and seek for my brothers."

And when the night came, she fled away and went straight into the wood. She went on all that night and the next day, until she could go no longer for weariness. At last she saw a rude hut, and she went in and found a room with six little beds in it; she did not dare to lie down in one, but she crept under one and lay on the hard boards and wished for night. When it was near the time of sun-setting she heard a rustling sound, and saw six swans come flying it at the window. They alighted on the ground, and blew at one an-other until they had blown all their feathers off, and then they stripped off their swan-skin as if it had been a shirt. And the maid-en looked at them and knew them for her brothers, and was very glad, and crept from under the bed. The brothers were not less glad when their sister appeared, but their joy did not last long.

"You must not stay here," said they to her; "this is a robbers' haunt, and if they were to come and find you here, they would kill you."

"And cannot you defend me?" asked the little sister.

"No," answered they, "for we can only get rid of our swan-skins and keep our human shape every evening for a quarter of an hour, but after that we must be changed again into swans."

Their sister wept at hearing this, and said, "Can nothing be done to set you free?"

"Oh no," answered they, "the work would be too hard for you. For six whole years you would be obliged never to speak or laugh, and make during that time six little shirts out of aster-flowers. If you were to let fall a single word before the work was ended, all would be of no good."

And just as the brothers had finished telling her this, the quarter of an hour came to an end, and they changed into swans and flew out of the window.

But the maiden made up her mind to set her brothers free, even though it should cost her her life. She left the hut, and going into the middle of the wood, she climbed a tree, and there passed the night. The next morning she set to work and gathered asters and began sewing them together: as for speaking, there was no one to speak to, and as for laughing, she had no mind to it; so she sat on and looked at nothing but her work. When she had been going on like this for a long time, it happened that the king of that country went a-hunting in the wood, and some of his huntsmen came up to the tree in which the maiden sat. They called out to her, saying, "Who art thou?" But she gave no answer. "Come down," cried they; "we will do thee no harm." But she only shook her head. And when they tormented her further with questions she threw down to them her gold necklace, hoping they would be content with that. But they would not leave off, so she threw down to them her girdle, and when that was no good, her garters, and one after another everything she had on and could possibly spare, until she had nothing left but her smock. But all was no good, the huntsmen would not be put off any longer, and they climbed the tree, carried the maiden off, and brought her to the king. The king asked, "Who art thou? What wert thou doing in the tree?" But she answered nothing. He spoke to her in all the languages he knew, but she remained dumb: but, being very beautiful, the king inclined to her, and he felt a great love rise up in his heart towards her; and casting his mantle round her, he put her before him on his horse and brought her to his castle. Then he caused rich clothing to be put upon her, and her beauty shone as bright as the morning, but no word would she utter. He seated her by his side at table, and her modesty and gentle mien so pleased him, that he said, "This maiden I choose for wife, and no other in all the world," and accordingly after a few days they were married.

But the king had a wicked mother, who

was displeased with the marriage, and spoke ill of the young queen.

"Who knows where the maid can have come from?" said she, "and not able to speak a word! She is not worthy of a king!"

After a year had passed, and the queen brought her first child into the world, the old woman carried it away, and marked the queen's mouth with blood as she lay sleeping. Then she went to the king and declared that his wife was an eater of human flesh. The king would not believe such a thing, and ordered that no one should do her any harm. And the queen went on quietly sewing the shirts and caring for nothing else. The next time that a fine boy was born, the wicked step-mother used the same deceit, but the king would give no credence to her words, for he said, "She is too tender and good to do any such thing, and if she were only not dumb, and could justify herself, then her innocence would be as clear as day."

When for the third time the old woman stole away the new-born child and accused the queen, who was unable to say a word in her defense, the king could do no other but give her up to justice, and she was sentenced to suffer death by fire.

The day on which her sentence was to be carried out was the very last one of the sixth year of the years during which she had neither spoken nor laughed, to free her dear

brothers from the evil spell. The six shirts
were ready, all except one which wanted the
left sleeve. And when she was led to the pile
of wood, she carried the six shirts on her
arm, and when she mounted the pile and the
fire was about to be kindled, all at once she
cried out aloud, for there were six swans
coming flying through the air; and she saw

that her deliverance was near, and her heart beat for joy. The swans came close up to her with rushing wings, and stooped round her, so that she could throw the shirts over them; and when that had been done the swan-skins fell off them, and her brothers stood before her in their own bodies quite safe and sound; but as one shirt wanted the left sleeve, so the youngest brother had a swan's wing instead of a left arm. They embraced and kissed each other, and the queen went up to the king, who looked on full of astonishment, and began to speak to him and to say, "Dearest husband, now I may dare to speak and tell you that I am innocent, and have been falsely accused," and she related to him the treachery of the step-mother, who had taken away the three children and hidden them. And she was reconciled to the king with great joy, while the wicked woman was bound to the stake on the pile of wood and burnt to ashes.

And the king and queen lived many years with their six brothers in peace and joy.

here lived once an old queen, whose husband had been dead many years. She had a beautiful daughter who was promised in marriage to a king's son living a great way off. When the time appointed for the wedding drew near, and the old queen had to send her daughter into the foreign land, she got together many costly things, furniture and cups and jewels and adornments, both of gold and silver, everything proper for the dowry of a royal princess, for she loved her daughter dearly. She gave her also a waiting gentle-woman to attend her and to give her into the bridegroom's hands; and they were each to have a horse for the journey, and the princess's horse was named Falada, and he could speak. When the time for parting came, the old queen took her daughter to her chamber, and with a little knife she cut her own finger so that it bled; and she held beneath it a white napkin, and on it fell three drops of blood; and she gave it to her daughter, bidding her take care of it, for it would be needful to her on the way. Then they took leave of each other; and the prin-

cess put the napkin in her bosom, got on her horse, and set out to go to the bridegroom. After she had ridden an hour, she began to feel very thirsty, and she said to the waiting-woman, "Get down, and fill my cup that you are carrying with water from the brook; I have great desire to drink."

"Get down yourself," said the waiting-woman, "and if you are thirsty, stoop down and drink; I will not be your slave."

And as her thirst was so great, the princess had to get down and to stoop and drink of the water of the brook, and could not have her gold cup to serve her. "Oh dear!" said the poor princess. And the three drops of blood heard her, and said, "If your mother knew of this, it would break her heart."

But the princess answered nothing, and quietly mounted her horse again. So they rode on some miles farther; the day was warm, the sun shone hot, and the princess grew thirsty once more. And when they came to a water-course she called again to the waiting-woman and said, "Get down, and give me to drink out of my golden cup." For she had forgotten all that had gone before. But the waiting-woman spoke still more scornfully and said, "If you want a drink, you may get it yourself; I am not going to be your slave."

So, as her thirst was so great, the princess had to get off her horse and to stoop towards the running water to drink, and as she stooped, she wept and said, "Oh dear!" And the three drops of blood heard her and answered, "If your mother knew of this, it would break her heart!"

And as she drank and stooped over, the napkin on which were the three drops of blood fell out of her bosom and floated down the stream, and in her distress she never noticed it; not so the waiting-woman, who rejoiced because she should have power over the bride, who, now that she had lost the three drops of blood, had become weak, and unable to defend herself. And when she was going to mount her horse again the waiting-woman cried, "Falada belongs to me, and this jade to you." And the princess had to give way and let it be as she said. Then the waiting-woman ordered the princess with many hard words to take off her rich clothing and to put on her plain garments, and then she made her swear to say nothing of the matter when they came to the royal court; threatening to take her life if she refused. And all the while Falada noticed and remembered.

The waiting-woman then mounting Falada, and the princess the sorry jade, they journeyed on till they reached the royal castle. There was great joy at their coming, and the king's son hastened to meet them, and lifted the waiting woman from her horse, thinking she was his bride; and then he led her up the stairs, while the real princess had to remain below. But the old king, who was looking out of the window, saw her standing in the yard, and noticed how delicate and gentle and beautiful she was, and then he went down and asked the seeming bride who it was that she had brought with her and that was now standing in the courtyard.

"Oh!" answered the bride, "I only brought her with me for company; give the maid something to do, that she may not be for ever standing idle."

But the old king had no work to give her; until he bethought him of a boy he had who took care of the geese, and that she might help him. And so the real princess was sent to keep geese with the goose boy, who was called Conrad.

Soon after the false bride said to the prince, "Dearest husband, I pray thee do me a pleasure."

"With all my heart," answered he.

"Then" said she, "send for the knacker, that he may carry off the horse I came here upon, and make away with him; he was very troublesome to me on the journey." For she was afraid that the horse might tell how she had behaved to the princess. And when the order had been given that Falada should die, it came to the princess's ears, and she came to the knacker's man secretly, and promised him a piece of gold if he would do her a service. There was in the town a great dark gate-way through which she had to pass morning and evening with her geese, and she asked the man to take Falada's head and to nail it on the gate, that she might always see it as she passed by. And the man promised, and he took Falada's head and nailed it fast in the dark gate-way.

Early next morning as she and Conrad drove their geese through the gate, she said as she went by,

"O Falada, dost thou hang there?"

And the head answered,

"Princess, dost thou so meanly fare?
But if thy mother knew thy pain,
Her heart would surely break in twain."

But she went on through the town, driving her geese to the field. And when they came into the meadows, she sat down and undid her hair, which was all of gold, and when Conrad saw how it glistened, he wanted to pull out a few hairs for himself. And she said,

"O wind, blow Conrad's hat away,
Make him run after as it flies,
While I wish my gold hair will play,
And twist it up in seemly wise."

Then there came a wind strong enough to blow Conrad's hat far away over the fields, and he had to run after it; and by the time he came back she had put up her hair with combs and pins, and he could not get at any to pull it out; and he was sulky and would not speak to her; so they looked after the geese until the evening came, and then they went home.

The next morning, as they passed under the dark gate-way, the princess said,

"O Falada, dost thou hang there?"

And Falada answered,

"Princess, dost thou so meanly fare?
But if they mother knew thy pain,
Her heart would surely break in twain."

And when they reached the fields she sat down and began to comb out her hair; then Conrad came up and wanted to seize upon some of it, and she cried,

"O wind, blow Conrad's hat away,
Make him run after as it flies,
While I with my gold hair will play,
And do it up in seemly wise."

Then the wind came and blew Conrad's hat very far away, so that he had to run after it, and when it came back again her hair was put up again, so that he could pull none of it out; and they tended the geese until the evening.

And after they had got home, Conrad went to the old king and said, "I will tend the geese no longer with that girl!"

"Why not?" asked the old king.

"Because she vexes me the whole day long," answered Conrad. Then the old king ordered him to tell how it was.

"Every morning," said Conrad, "as we pass under the dark gate-way with the geese, there is an old horse's head hanging on the wall, and she says to it,

'O Falada, dost thou hang there?'

And the head answers,

> *'Princess, dost thou so meanly fare?*
> *But if thy mother knew thy pain,*
> *Her heart would surely break in twain.'"*

And besides this, Conrad related all that happened in the fields, and how he was obliged to run after his hat.

The old king told him to go to drive the geese next morning as usual, and he himself went behind the gate and listened how the maiden spoke to Falada; and then he followed them into the fields, and hid himself behind a bush; and he watched the goose-boy and the goose-girl tend the geese; and after a while he saw the girl make her hair all loose, and how it gleamed and shone. Soon she said,

> *"O wind, blow Conrad's hat away,*
> *And make him follow as it flies,*
> *While I with my gold hair will play,*
> *And bind it up in seemly wise."*

Then there came a gust of wind and away went Conrad's hat, and he after it, while the maiden combed and bound up her hair; and the old king saw all that went on. At last he went unnoticed away, and when the goose-girl came back in the evening he sent for her, and asked the reason of her doing all this.

"That I dare not tell you," she answered, "nor can I tell any man of my woe, for when I was in danger of my life I swore an oath not to reveal it." And he pressed her sore, and left her no peace, but he could get nothing out of her. At last he said, "If you will not tell it me, tell it to the iron oven," and went away. Then she crept into the iron oven, and began to weep and to lament, and at last she opened her heart and said, "Here I sit forsaken of all the world, and I am a king's daughter, and a wicked waiting-woman forced me to give up my royal garments and my place at the bridegroom's side, and I am made a goose-girl, and have to do mean service. And if my mother knew, it would break her heart."

Now the old king was standing outside by the oven-door listening, and he heard all she said, and he called to her and told her to come out of the oven. And he caused royal clothing to be put upon her, and it was a marvel to see how beautiful she was. The old king then called his son and proved to him that he had the wrong bride, for she was

really only a waiting-woman, and that the true bride was here at hand, she who had been the goose-girl. The prince was glad at heart when he saw her beauty and gentleness; and a great feast was made ready, and all the court people and good friends were bidden to it. The bridegroom sat in the midst with the princess on one side and the waiting-woman on the other; and the false bride did not know the true one, because she was dazzled with her glittering braveries. When all the company had eaten and drunk and were merry, the old king gave the waiting-woman a question to answer, as to what such a one deserved, who had deceived her masters in such and such a manner, telling the whole story, and ending by asking, "Now, what doom does such a one deserve?"

"No better than this," answered the false bride, "that she be put naked into a cask, studded inside with sharp nails, and be dragged along in it by two white horses from street to street, until she be dead."

"Thou hast spoken thy own doom," said the old king; "as thou hast said, so shall it be done." And when the sentence was fulfulled, the prince married the true bride, and ever after they ruled over their kingdom in peace and blessedness.

The brother took his sister's hand and said to her, "Since our mother died we have had no good days; our stepmother beats us every day, and if we go near her she kicks us away; we have nothing to eat but hard crusts of bread left over; the dog under the table fares better; he gets a good piece every now and then. If our mother only knew, how she would pity us! Come, let us go together out into the wide world!"

So they went, and journeyed the whole day through fields and meadows and stony places, and if it rained the sister said, "The skies and we are weeping together."

In the evening they came to a great wood, and they were so weary with hunger and their long journey, that they climbed up into a high tree and fell asleep.

The next morning, when they awoke, the sun was high in heaven, and shone brightly through the leaves. Then said the brother, "Sister, I am thirsty; if I only knew where to find a brook, that I might go and drink! I almost think that I hear one rushing." So the brother got down and led his sister by the hand, and they went to seek the brook. But their wicked stepmother was a witch, and had known quite well that the two children had run away, and had sneaked after them, as only witches can, and had laid a spell on all the brooks in the forest. So when they found a little stream flowing smoothly over its pebbles, the brother was going to drink of it; but the sister heard how it said in its rushing,

"He a tiger will be who drinks of me,
Who drinks of me a tiger will be!"

Then the sister cried, "Pray, dear brother, do not drink, or you will become a wild beast, and will tear me in pieces."

So the brother refrained from drinking, though his thirst was great, and he said he would wait till he came to the next brook. When they came to a second brook the sister heard it say,

"He a wolf will be who drinks of me,
Who drinks of me a wolf will be!"

Then the sister cried, "Pray, dear brother, do not drink, or you will be turned into a wolf, and will eat me up!"

So the brother refrained from drinking, and said, "I will wait until we come to the next brook, and then I must drink, whatever you say; my thirst is so great."

And when they came to the third brook the sister heard how in its rushing it said,

"Who drinks of me a fawn will be,
He a fawn will be who drinks of me!"

Then the sister said, "O my brother, I pray

. . . as the first drops passed his lips he became a fawn. (page 193)

drink not, or you will be turned into a fawn, and run away far from me."

But he had already kneeled by the side of the brook and stopped and drunk of the water, and as the first drops passed his lips he became a fawn.

And the sister wept over her poor lost brother, and the fawn wept also, and stayed sadly beside her. At last the maiden said, "Be comforted, dear fawn, indeed I will never leave you."

Then she untied her golden girdle and bound it round the fawn's neck, and went and gathered rushes to make a soft cord, which she fastened to him; and then she led him on, and they went deeper into the forest. And when they had gone a long way, they came at last to a little house, and the maiden looked inside, and as it was empty she thought, "We might as well live here."

And she fetched leaves and moss to make a soft bed for the fawn, and every morning she went out and gathered roots and berries and nuts for herself, and fresh grass for the fawn, who ate out of her hand with joy, frolicking round her. At night, when the sister was tired, and had said her prayers, she laid her head on the fawn's back, which served her for a pillow, and softly fell asleep. And if only the brother could have got back his own shape again, it would have been a charming life. So they lived a long while in the wilderness alone.

Now it happened that the king of that country held a great hunt in the forest. The blowing of the horns, the barking of the dogs, and the lusty shouts of the huntsmen sounded through the wood, and the fawn heard them and was eager to be among them.

"Oh," said he to his sister, "do let me go to the hunt; I cannot stay behind any longer," and begged so long that at last she consented.

"But mind," she said to him, "come back to me at night. I must lock my door against the wild hunters, so, in order that I may know you, you must knock and say, 'Little sister, let me in,' and unless I hear that I shall not unlock the door."

Then the fawn sprang out, and felt glad and merry in the open air. The king and his huntsmen saw the beautiful animal, and began at once to pursue him, but they could not come within reach of him, for when they thought they were certain of him he sprang away over the bushes and disappeared. As soon as it was dark he went back to the little house, knocked at the door, and said, "Little sister, let me in."

Then the door was opened to him, and he went in, and rested the whole night long on his soft bed. The next morning the hunt began anew, and when the fawn heard the hunting-horns and the tally-ho of the huntsmen he could rest no longer, and said,

"Little sister, let me out, I must go." The sister opened the door and said, "Now, mind you must come back at night and say the same words."

When the king and his hunters saw the fawn with the golden collar again, they chased him closely, but he was too nimble and swift for them. This lasted the whole day, and at last the hunters surrounded him, and one of them wounded his foot a little, so that he was obliged to limp and to go slowly. Then a hunter slipped after him to the little house, and heard how he called out, "Little sister, let me in," and saw the door open and shut again after him directly. The hunter noticed all this carefully, went to the king, and told him all he had seen and heard. Then said the king, "Tomorrow we will hunt again."

But the sister was very terrified when she saw that her fawn was wounded. She washed his foot, laid cooling leaves round it, and said, "Lie down on your bed, dear fawn, and rest, that you may be soon well." The wound was very slight, so that the fawn felt nothing of it the next morning. And when he heard the noise of the hunting outside, he said, "I cannot stay in, I must go after them; I shall not be taken easily again!" The sister began to weep, and said, "I know you will be killed, and I left alone here in the forest, and forsaken of everybody. I cannot let you go!"

"Then I shall die here with longing,"

answered the fawn; "when I hear the sound of the horn I feel as if I should leap out of my skin."

Then the sister, seeing there was no help for it, unlocked the door with a heavy heart, and the fawn bounded away into the forest, well and merry. When the king saw him, he said to his hunters, "Now, follow him up all day long till the night comes, and see that you do him no hurt."

So as soon as the sun had gone down, the king said to the huntsman: "Now, come and show me the little house in the wood."

And when he got to the door he knocked at it, and cried, "Little sister, let me in!"

Then the door opened, and the king went in, and there stood a maiden more beautiful than any he had seen before. The maiden shrieked out when she saw, instead of the fawn, a man standing there with a gold crown on his head. But the king looked kindly on her, took her by the hand, and said, "Will you go with me to my castle, and be my dear wife?"

"Oh yes," answered the maiden, "but the fawn must come too. I could not leave him." And the king said, "He shall remain with you as long as you live, and shall lack nothing." Then the fawn came bounding in, and the sister tied the cord of rushes to him, and led him by her own hand out of the little house.

The king put the beautiful maiden on his

horse, and carried her to his castle, where the wedding was held with great pomp; so she became lady queen, and they lived together happily for a long while; the fawn was well tended and cherished, and he gambolled about the castle garden.

Now the wicked stepmother, whose fault it was that the children were driven out into the world, never dreamed but that the sister had been eaten up by wild beasts in the forest, and that the brother, in the likeness of a fawn, had been slain by the hunters. But when she heard that they were so happy, and that things had gone so well with them, jealousy and envy arose in her heart, and left her no peace, and her chief thought was how to bring misfortune upon them.

Her own daughter, who was as ugly as sin, and had only one eye, complained to her, and said, "I never had the chance of being a queen."

"Never mind," said the old woman, to satisfy her; "when the time comes, I shall be at hand."

After a while the queen brought a beautiful baby-boy into the world, and that day the king was out hunting. The old witch took the shape of the bedchamber woman, and went into the room where the queen lay, and said to her, "Come, the bath is ready; it will give you refreshment and new strength. Quick, or it will be cold."

Her daughter was within call, so they carried the sick queen into the bath-room, and left her there. And in the bath-room they had made a great fire, so as to suffocate the beautiful young queen.

When that was managed, the old woman took her daughter, put a cap on her, and laid her in the bed in the queen's place, gave her also the queen's form and countenance, only she could not restore the lost eye. So, in order that the king might not remark it, she had to lie on the side where there was no eye. In the evening, when the king came home and heard that a little son was born to him, he rejoiced with all his heart, and was going at once to his dear wife's bedside to see how she did. Then the old woman cried hastily, "For your life, do not draw back the curtains, to let in the light upon her; she must be kept quiet." So the king went away, and never knew that a false queen was lying in the bed.

Now, when it was midnight, and everyone was asleep, the nurse, who was sitting by the cradle in the nursery and watching there alone, saw the door open, and the true queen come in. She took the child out of the cradle, laid it in her bosom, and fed it. Then she shook out its little pillow, put the child back again, and covered it with the coverlet. She did not forget the fawn either: she went to him where he lay in the corner, and stroked his back tenderly. Then she went in perfect silence out at the door, and the nurse next morning asked the watchmen if any one had entered the castle during the night, but they said they had seen no one. And the queen came many nights, and never said a word; the nurse saw her always, but she did not dare speak of it to anyone.

After some time had gone by in this manner, the queen seemed to find voice, and said one night,

"My child my fawn twice more I come to see,
Twice more I come, and then the end must be."

The nurse said nothing, but as soon as the queen had disappeared she went to the king and told him all. The king said, "Ah, heaven! what do I hear! I will myself watch by the child tomorrow night."

So at evening he went into the nursery, and at midnight the queen appeared, and said,

"My child my fawn once more I come to see,
Once more I come, and then the end must be."

And she tended the child, as she was accustomed to do, before she vanished. The king dared not speak to her, but he watched again the following night, and heard her say,

"My child my fawn this once I come to see,
This once I come, and now the end must be."

Then the king could contain himself no longer, but rushed towards her, saying, "You are no other than my dear wife!" Then she answered, "Yes, I am your dear wife," and in that moment, by the grace of heaven, her life returned to her, and she was once more well and strong. Then she told the king the snare that the wicked witch and her daughter had laid for her. The king had them both brought to judgment, and sentence was passed upon them. The daughter was sent away into the wood, where she was devoured by the wild beasts, and the witch was burned, and ended miserably. And as soon as her body was in ashes the spell was removed from the fawn, and he took human shape again; and then the sister and brother lived happily together until the end.

ne summer morn-
ing a little tai-
lor was sitting on
his board near the
window, and work-
ing cheerfully
with all his might, when an old
woman came down the street
crying, "Good jelly to sell! good jelly to
sell!"

The cry sounded pleasant in the little
tailor's ears, so he put his head out of the
window, and called out, "Here, my good
woman—come here, if you want a customer."

So the poor woman climbed the steps with
her heavy basket, and was obliged to unpack
and display all her pots to the tailor. He
looked at every one of them, and lifting all
the lids, applied his nose to each, and said at
last, "The jelly seems pretty good; you may
weigh me out four half ounces, or I don't
mind having a quarter of a pound."

The woman, who had expected to find a
good customer, gave him what he asked for,
but went off angry and grumbling.

"This jelly is the very thing for me," cried
the little tailor; "it will give me strength and
cunning;" and he took down the bread from

the cupboard, cut a whole round of the loaf, and spread the jelly on it, laid it near him, and went on stitching more gallantly than ever. All the while the scent of the sweet jelly was spreading throughout the room, where there were quantities of flies, who were attracted by it and flew to partake.

"Now then, who asked you to come?" said the tailor, and drove the unbidden guests away. But the flies, not understanding his language, were not to be got rid of like that, and returned in larger numbers than before. Then the tailor, not being able to stand it any longer, took from his chimney-corner a ragged cloth, and saying, "Now, I'll let you have it!" beat it among them unmercifully. When he ceased, and counted the slain, he found seven lying dead before him.

"This is indeed somewhat," he said, wondering at his own gallantry; "the whole town shall know this."

So he hastened to cut out a belt, and he stitched it, and put on it in large capitals, "Seven at one blow!"

"—The town, did I say!" said the little tailor; "the whole world shall know it!" And his heart quivered with joy, like a lamb's tail.

The tailor fastened the belt round him, and began to think of going out into the world, for his workshop seemed too small for his worship. So he looked about in all the house for something that it would be useful to take with him, but he found nothing but an old cheese, which he put in his pocket. Outside the door he noticed that a bird had got caught in the bushes, so he took that and put it in his pocket with the cheese. Then he set out gallantly on his way, and as he was light and active he felt no fatigue. The way led over a mountain, and when he reached the topmost peak he saw a terrible giant sitting there, and looking about him at his ease. The tailor went bravely up to him, called out to him and said, "Comrade, good day! there you sit looking over the wide world! I am on the way thither to seek my fortune: have you a fancy to go with me?"

The giant looked at the tailor contemptuously, and said, "You little rascal! you miserable fellow!"

"That may be!" answered the little tailor, and undoing his coat he showed the giant his belt; "you can read there whether I am a man or not!"

The giant read: "Seven at one blow!" and thinking it meant men that the tailor had killed, felt at once more respect for the little fellow. But as he wanted to prove him, he took up a stone and squeezed it so hard that water came out of it.

"Now you can do that," said the giant, "that is, if you have the strength for it."

"That's not much," said the little tailor, "I call that play," and he put his hand in his pocket and took out the cheese and squeezed it, so that the whey ran out of it.

"Well," said he, "what do you think of that?"

The giant did not know what to say to it, for he could not have believed it of the little man. Then the giant took up a stone and threw it so high that it was nearly out of sight.

"Now, little fellow, suppose you do that!"

"Well thrown," said the tailor; "but the stone fell back to earth again,—I will throw you one that will never come back." So he felt in his pocket, took out the bird, and threw it into the air. And the bird, when it found itself at liberty, took wing, flew off, and returned no more.

"What do you think of that, comrade?" asked the tailor.

"There is no doubt that you can throw," said the giant; "but we will see if you can carry."

He led the little tailor to a mighty oak-tree which had been felled, and was lying on the ground, and said, "Now, if you are strong enough, help me to carry this tree out of the wood."

"Willingly," answered the little man; "you take the trunk on your shoulders, I will take the branches with all their foliage, that is much the most difficult."

So the giant took the trunk on his shoulders, and the tailor seated himself on a branch, and the giant, who could not see what he was doing, had the whole tree to carry, and the little man on it as well. And the little man was very cheerful and merry, and whistled the tune: *"There were three tailors riding by,"* as if carrying the tree was mere child's play. The giant, when he had struggled on under his heavy load a part of the way, was tired out, and cried, "Look here, I must let go the tree!"

The tailor jumped off quickly, and taking hold of the tree with both arms, as if he were carrying it, said to the giant, "You see you can't carry the tree though you are such a big fellow!"

They went on together a little farther, and presently they came to a cherry-tree, and the giant took hold of the topmost branches, where the ripest fruit hung, and pulling them downwards, gave them to the tailor to hold, bidding him eat. But the little tailor was much too weak to hold the tree, and as the giant let go, the tree sprang back, and the tailor was caught up into the air. And when he dropped down again without any damage, the giant said to him, "How is this? haven't you strength enough to hold such a weak sprig as that?"

"It is not strength that is lacking," answered the little tailor; "how should it to one who has slain seven at one blow! I just jumped over the tree because the hunters are shooting down there in the bushes. You jump it too, if you can."

The giant made the attempt, and not being

able to vault the tree, he remained hanging in the branches, so that once more the little tailor got the better of him. Then said the giant, "As you are such a gallant fellow, suppose you come with me to our den, and stay the night."

The tailor was quite willing, and he followed him. When they reached the den there sat some other giants by the fire, and each had a roasted sheep in his hand, and was eating it. The little tailor looked round and thought, "There is more elbow-room here than in my workshop."

And the giant showed him a bed, and told him he had better lie down upon it and go to sleep. The bed was, however, too big for the tailor, so he did not stay in it, but crept into a corner to sleep. As soon as it was midnight the giant got up, took a great staff of iron and beat the bed through with one stroke, and supposed he had made an end of that grasshopper of a tailor. Very early in the morning the giants went into the wood and forgot all about the little tailor, and when they saw him coming after them alive and merry, they were terribly frightened, and, thinking he was going to kill them, they ran away in all haste.

So the little tailor marched on, always following his nose. And after he had gone a great way he entered the courtyard belonging to a king's palace, and there he felt so overpowered with fatigue that he lay down and fell asleep. In the meanwhile came various people, who looked at him very curiously, and read on his belt, "Seven at one blow!"

"Oh!" said they, "why should this great lord come here in time of peace? what a mighty champion he must be."

Then they went and told the king about him, and they thought that if war should break out what a worthy and useful man he would be, and that he ought not to be allowed to depart at any price. The king then summoned his council, and sent one of his courtiers to the little tailor to beg him, so soon as he should wake up, to consent to serve in the king's army. So the messenger stood and waited at the sleeper's side until his limbs began to stretch, and his eyes to open, and then he carried his answer back. And the answer was, "That was the reason for which I came," said the little tailor. "I am ready to enter the king's service."

So he was received into it very honorably, and a separate dwelling set apart for him.

But the rest of the soldiers were very much set against the little tailor, and they wished him a thousand miles away.

"What shall be done about it?" they said among themselves; "if we pick a quarrel and fight with him, then seven of us will fall at each blow. That will be of no good to us."

So they came to a resolution, and went all

together to the king to ask for their discharge.

"We never intended," said they, "to serve with a man who kills seven at a blow."

The king felt sorry to lose all his faithful servants because of one man, and he wished that he had never seen him, and would willingly get rid of him if he might. But he did not dare to dismiss the little tailor for fear he should kill all the king's people, and place himself upon the throne. He thought a long while about it, and at last made up his mind what to do. He sent for the little tailor, and told him that as he was so great a warrior he had a proposal to make to him. He told him that in a wood in his dominions dwelt two giants, who did great damage by robbery, murder, and fire, and that no man durst go near them for fear of his life. But that if the tailor should overcome and slay both these giants the king would give him his only daughter in marriage, and half his kingdom as dowry, and that a hundred horsemen should go with him to give him assistance.

"That would be something for a man like me!" thought the little tailor, "a beautiful princess and half a kingdom are not to be had every day," and he said to the king, "Oh yes, I can soon overcome the giants, and yet have no need of the hundred horsemen; he who can kill seven at one blow has no need to be afraid of two."

So the little tailor set out, and the hundred

horsemen followed him. When he came to the border of the wood he said to his escort, "Stay here while I go to attack the giants."

Then he sprang into the wood, and looked about him right and left. After a while he caught sight of the two giants; they were lying down under a tree asleep, and snoring so that all the branches shook. The little tailor, all alive, filled both his pockets with stones and climbed up into the tree, and made his way to an overhanging bough, so that he could seat himself just above the sleepers; and from there he let one stone after another fall on the chest of one of the giants. For a long time the giant was quite unaware of this, but at last he woke up and pushed his comrade, and said, "What are you hitting me for?"

"You are dreaming," said the other, "I am not touching you." And they composed themselves again to sleep, and the tailor let fall a stone on the other giant.

"What can that be?" cried he, "what are you casting at me?"

"I am casting nothing at you," answered the first, grumbling.

They disputed about it for a while, but as they were tired, they gave it up at last, and their eyes closed once more. Then the little tailor began his game anew, picked out a heavier stone and threw it down with force upon the first giant's chest.

"This is too much!" cried he, and sprang

up like a madman and struck his companion such a blow that the tree shook above them. The other paid him back with ready coin, and they fought with such fury that they tore up trees by their roots to use for weapons against each other, so that at last they both of them lay dead upon the ground. And now the little tailor got down.

"Another piece of luck!" said he,—"that the tree I was sitting in did not get torn up too, or else I should have had to jump like a squirrel from one tree to another."

Then he drew his sword and gave each of the giants a few hacks in the breast, and went back to the horsemen and said, "The deed is done, I have made an end of both of them: but it went hard with me, in the struggle they rooted up trees to defend themselves, but it was of no use, they had to do with a man who can kill seven at one blow."

"Then are you not wounded?" asked the horsemen.

"Nothing of the sort!" answered the tailor, "I have not turned a hair."

The horsemen still would not believe it, and rode into the wood to see, and there they found the giants wallowing in their blood, and all about them lying the uprooted trees.

The little tailor then claimed the promised boon, but the king repented him of his offer, and he sought again how to rid himself of the hero.

"Before you can possess my daughter and the half of my kingdom," said he to the tailor, "you must perform another heroic act. In the wood lives a unicorn who does great damage; you must secure him."

"A unicorn does not strike more terror into me than two giants. Seven at one blow!—that is my way," was the tailor's answer.

So, taking a rope and an axe with him, he went out into the wood, and told those who were ordered to attend him to wait outside. He had not far to seek, the unicorn soon came out and sprang at him, as if he would make an end of him without delay. "Softly, softly," said he, "most haste, worst speed," and remained standing until the animal came quite near, then he slipped quietly behind a tree. The unicorn ran with all his might against the tree and stuck his horn so deep into the trunk that he could not get it out again, and so was taken.

"Now I have you," said the tailor, coming out from behind the tree, and, putting the rope round the unicorn's neck, he took the axe, set free the horn, and when all his party were assembled he led forth the animal and brought it to the king.

The king did not yet wish to give him the promised reward, and set him a third task to do. Before the wedding could take place the tailor was to secure a wild boar which had done a great deal of damage in the wood.

The huntsmen were to accompany him.

"All right," said the tailor, "this is child's play."

But he did not take the huntsmen into the wood, and they were all the better pleased, for the wild boar had many a time before received them in such a way that they had no fancy to disturb him. When the boar caught sight of the tailor he ran at him with foaming mouth and gleaming tusks to bear him to the ground, but the nimble hero rushed into a chapel which chanced to be near, and jumped quickly out of a window on the other side. The boar ran after him, and when he got inside the door shut after him, and there he was imprisoned, for the creature was too big and unwieldy to jump out of the window too. Then the little tailor called the huntsmen that they might see the prisoner with their own eyes; and then he betook himself to the king, who now, whether he liked it or not, was obliged to fulfill his promise, and give him his daughter and the half of his kingdom. But if he had known that the great warrior was only a little tailor he would have taken it still more to heart. So the wedding was celebrated with great splendor and little joy, and the tailor was made into a king.

One night the young queen heard her husband talking in his sleep and saying, "Now boy, make me that waistcoat and patch me those breeches, or I will lay my yard measure about your shoulders!"

And so, as she perceived of what low birth her husband was, she went to her father the next morning and told him all, and begged him to set her free from a man who was nothing better than a tailor. The king bade her be comforted, saying, "To-night leave your bedroom door open, my guard shall stand outside, and when he is asleep they shall come in and bind him and carry him off to a ship, and he shall be sent to the other side of the world."

So the wife felt consoled, but the king's water-bearer, who had been listening all the while, went to the little tailor and disclosed to him the whole plan.

"I shall put a stop to all this," said he.

At night he lay down as usual in bed, and when his wife thought that he was asleep, she got up, opened the door and lay down again. The little tailor, who only made believe to be asleep, began to murmur plainly, "Now, boy, make me that waistcoat and patch me those breeches, or I will lay my yard measure about your shoulders! I have slain seven at one blow, killed two giants, caught a unicorn, and taken a wild boar, and shall I be afraid of those who are standing outside my room door?"

And when they heard the tailor say this, a great fear seized them; they fled away as if they had been wild hares, and none of them would venture to attack him.

And so the little tailor all his lifetime remained a king.

here was once a soldier who had served the king faithfully for many years, but when the war was over and he could serve no longer because of his many wounds, the king said to him: "You can go home. I don't need you any more. You won't be getting any more money, because when I pay wages I expect something in return." The soldier was very sad, for he couldn't see how he was going to keep body and soul together. With a heavy heart he left the king and walked all day until he came to a forest. As night was falling, he saw a light and headed for it. Soon he came to a house that belonged to a witch. "Give me a night's lodging and something to eat and drink," he said, "or I shall die." "Oho!" said she. "Who gives a runaway soldier anything? But I'll be merciful and take you in, if you'll do what I tell you." "And what may that be?" "To spade up my garden tomorrow." The soldier accepted her proposition and worked hard all the next day, but by the time he had finished, night was falling. "Hmm," said the witch. "I see that you can't start out today. I'll keep you

another night, but in return you must chop and split a cord of wood for me." That took the soldier all day and at nightfall the witch asked him to stay the night. "I have only a little thing to ask of you tomorrow," she said. "There's an old dry well behind the house. My light has fallen into it. It burns blue and never goes out. I want you to go down and get it for me." Next day the old woman took him to the well and let him down in a basket. He found the blue light and gave the signal for her to pull him up. She pulled him up all right, but when he was just below the rim she held out her hand and wanted him to give her the blue light. "Oh no," he said, for he read her wicked thoughts. "I won't give you the light until I have both my feet on the ground." At that the witch flew into a rage, let him drop to the bottom, and went away.

The ground at the bottom was moist and the poor soldier's fall didn't hurt him. The blue light was still burning, but what was the good of that? He was doomed to die, and he knew it. For a while he just sat there, feeling very dejected. Then he happened to put his hand in his pocket and felt his pipe, which was still half full of tobacco. "My last pleasure on earth!" he said to himself, took out the pipe, lit it with the blue light and began to smoke. The smoke rose in a ring and suddenly a black dwarf stood before him. "Master," said the dwarf, "what do you command?" The soldier was amazed. "What

He was doomed to die, and he knew it. (page 216)

am I supposed to command?" he asked. "I must do whatever you ask," said the dwarf. "That's fine," said the soldier. "Then first of all, help me out of this well." The dwarf took him by the hand and led him through an underground passage, and the soldier didn't forget to take the blue light with him. On the way the dwarf showed him all the treasures the witch had amassed and hidden there, and the soldier took as much gold as he could carry. When he was back above ground, he said to the dwarf: "Now go and tie up the old witch and take her to jail." A second later bloodcurdling screams were heard. She rode past as quick as the wind on the back of a wildcat, and a short while later the dwarf came back. "Your orders have been carried out," he announced. "She's already hanging on the gallows. What else do you command, master?" "Nothing right now. You can go home, but be ready when I call you." "All you have to do," said the dwarf, "is light your pipe with the blue light. I'll be there before you know it." And at that he vanished.

The soldier went back to the town he had come from. He stopped at the best inn, had fine clothes made, and ordered the inn-keeper to furnish his room as splendidly as possible. When the room was ready and the soldier had moved in, he called the black dwarf and said: "I served the king faithfully, but he sent me away and let me go hungry. Now I'm going to get even." "What should I do?" asked the dwarf. "Late tonight, when the king's daughter is asleep in her bed, bring her here without waking her. I'm going to make her work as my slavey." "That will be easy for me, but dangerous for you," said the dwarf. "If you're discovered, you'll be in hot water." At the stroke of twelve the door opened and the dwarf carried the king's daughter in. "Aha!" said the soldier. "So there you are. Well, get to work. Go get the broom and sweep the place out." When she had finished, he called her over to where he was sitting, stretched out his legs, and said: "Pull my boots off." When she had pulled them off, he threw them in her face, and she had to pick them up, clean them, and polish them until they shone. Only half-opening her eyes, she obeyed his commands without a murmur. At first cockcrow the dwarf carried her back to her bed in the royal palace.

When the king's daughter got up in the morning, she went to her father and told him she had had a strange dream. "I was carried through the streets with the speed of lightning and taken to the room of a soldier. I had to be his slavey and do all the nasty work and sweep the room and clean his boots. It was only a dream, but I'm as tired as if I'd really done it all." "Your dream may have been true," said the king. "Here's my advice. Fill your pocket with peas and make a little hole in it. If they carry you off again, the peas will fall out and leave a trail on the street." When the king said this, the dwarf, who had made himself invisible, was standing right there and he heard it all. That night when he carried the king's daughter through the streets again, some peas did indeed fall out of her pocket, but they couldn't make a trail, because the crafty dwarf had strewn peas in all the streets beforehand. And again the king's daughter had to do slavey's work until cock-crow.

Next morning the king sent his men out to look for the trail, but they couldn't find it because in every street, all over town, children were picking up peas and saying: "Last night it rained peas." "We'll have to think of something else," said the king. "Keep your shoes on when you go to bed. And before you come back from that place, hide one of them. Never fear, I'll find it." The black dwarf heard the king's plan and that night when the soldier asked him once again to go and get the king's daughter, he advised against it. "I don't know of any way to thwart that scheme. If the shoe is found in your room, you'll really be in for it." "Do as you're told," said the soldier. And for the third time the king's daughter had to work as his slavey. But before the dwarf carried her back to the palace, she hid one of her shoes under the bed.

Next morning the king had the whole town searched for his daughter's shoe, and it was found in the soldier's room. The dwarf had implored the soldier to save himself, and he had left town in haste, but was soon caught and thrown into prison. In his hurry to escape he had forgotten his most precious possessions, the blue light and his gold, and all he had in his pocket was one ducat. As he was standing loaded with chains at the window of his prison cell, he saw an old friend passing, and tapped on the windowpane. When his friend came over to him, he said: "Do me a favor. Get me the little bundle I left at the inn. I'll give you a ducat." His friend ran to the inn and brought him his bundle. As soon as the soldier was alone, he lit his pipe with the light and the dwarf appeared. "Don't be afraid," said the dwarf. "Go where they take you, and let them do as they please. Just be sure to take the blue light with you." The next day the soldier was brought to trial and though he had done no evil the judge sentenced him to death. When he was led out to die, he asked the king for a last kindness. "What sort of kindness?" the king asked. "Let me smoke one last pipe on the way," said the soldier. "You can smoke three," said the king, "but don't expect me to spare your life." The soldier took out his pipe and lit it with the blue light. When a few rings of smoke had gone up, the dwarf appeared, holding a little cudgel. "What does my master command?" he asked. "Strike down those false judges and their henchmen, and don't spare the king who has treated me so badly." The dwarf raced back and forth like forked lightning and everybody his cudgel so much as touched fell to the ground and didn't dare to move. The king was so terrified that he begged for mercy and to preserve his bare life made over his kingdom to the soldier and gave him his daughter for his wife.

In times gone by there was a king who had at the back of his castle a beautiful pleasure-garden, in which stood a tree that bore golden apples. As the apples ripened they were counted, but one morning one was missing. Then the king was angry, and he ordered that watch should be kept about the tree every night. Now the king had three sons, and he sent the eldest to spend the whole night in the garden; so he watched till midnight, and then he could keep off sleep no longer, and in the morning another apple was missing. The second son had to watch the following night; but it fared no better, for when twelve o'clock had struck he went to sleep, and in the morning another apple was missing. Now came the turn of the third son to watch, and he was ready to do so; but the king had less trust in him, and believed he would acquit himself still worse than his brothers, but in the end he consented to let him try. So the young man lay down under the tree to watch, and resolved that sleep should not be master. When it struck twelve something came rushing through the air, and he saw in the moonlight a bird flying towards him, whose feathers glittered like gold. The bird perched upon the tree, and had already pecked off an apple, when the young man let fly an arrow at it. The bird flew away, but the arrow had struck its plumage, and one of its golden feathers fell to the ground: the young man picked it up, and taking it next morning to the king, told him what had happened in the night. The king called his council together, and all declared that such a feather was worth more than the whole kingdom.

"Since the feather is so valuable," said the king, "one is not enough for me; I must and will have the whole bird."

So the eldest son set off, and relying on his own cleverness he thought he should soon find the golden bird. When he had gone some distance he saw a fox sitting at the edge of a wood, and he pointed his gun at him. The fox cried out, "Do not shoot me, and I will give you good counsel. You are on your way to find the golden bird, and this evening you will come to a village, in which two taverns stand facing each other. One will be brightly lighted up, and there will be plenty of merriment going on inside; do not mind about that, but go into the other one, although it will look to you very uninviting."

"How can a silly beast give one any rational advice?" thought the king's son, and let fly at the fox, but missed him, and he stretched out his tail and ran quick into the wood. Then the young man went on his way, and towards evening he came to the village, and there stood the two taverns; in one singing and dancing was going on, the other looked quite dull and wretched. "I should be a fool," said he, "to go into that dismal place, while there is anything so good close by." So he went into the merry inn, and there lived in clover, quite forgetting the bird and his father, and all good counsel.

As time went on, and the eldest son never came home, the second son set out to seek the golden bird. He met with the fox, just as the eldest did, and received good advice from him without attending to it. And when he came to the two taverns, his brother was standing and calling to him at the window of one of them, out of which came sounds of merriment; so he could not resist, but went in and revelled to his heart's content.

And then, as time went on, the youngest son wished to go forth, and to try his luck, but his father would not consent.

"It would be useless," said he; "he is much less likely to find the bird than his brothers, and if any misfortune were to happen to him he would not know how to help himself; his wits are none of the best."

But at last, as there was no peace to be had, he let him go. By the side of the wood sat the fox, begged him to spare his life, and gave him good counsel. The young man was kind, and said, "Be easy, little fox, I will do you no harm."

"You shall not repent of it," answered the fox, "and that you may get there all the sooner, get up and sit on my tail."

And no sooner had he done so than the fox began to run, and off they went over stock and stone, so that the wind whistled in their hair. When they reached the village the young man got down, and, following the fox's advice, went into the mean-looking tavern, without hesitating, and there he passed a quiet night. The next morning, when he went out into the field, the fox, who was sitting there already, said, "I will tell you further what you have to do. Go straight on until you come to a castle, before which a great band of soldiers lie, but do not trouble yourself about them, for they will be all asleep and snoring; pass through them and forward into the castle, and go through all the rooms, until you come to one where there is a golden bird hanging in a wooden cage. Near at hand will stand empty a golden cage of state, but you must beware of taking the bird out of his ugly cage and putting him into the fine one; if you do so you will come to harm."

After he had finished saying this the fox stretched out his tail again, and the king's son sat him down upon it; then away they went over stock and stone, so that the wind whistled through their hair. And when the king's

son reached the castle he found everything
as the fox had said: and he at last entered the
room where the golden bird was hanging in
a wooden cage, while a golden one was standing by; the three golden apples too were in
the room. Then, thinking it foolish to let the
beautiful bird stay in that mean and ugly

cage, he opened the door of it, took hold of
it, and put it in the golden one. In the same
moment the bird uttered a piercing cry. The
soldiers awoke, rushed in, seized the king's
son and put him in prison. The next morning
he was brought before a judge, and, as he
confessed everything, condemned to death.
But the king said he would spare his life on
one condition, that he should bring him the
golden horse whose paces were swifter than
the wind, and that then he should also receive the golden bird as a reward.

So the king's son set off to find the golden

horse, but he sighed, and was very sad, for how should it be accomplished? And then he saw his old friend the fox sitting by the road-side.

"Now, you see," said the fox, "all this has happened, because you would not listen to me. But be of good courage, I will bring you through, and will tell you how you are to get the golden horse. You must go straight on until you come to a castle, where the horse stands in his stable; before the stable-door the grooms will be lying, but they will all be asleep and snoring; and you can go and quietly lead out the horse. But one thing you must mind—take care to put upon him the plain saddle of wood and leather, and not the golden one, which will hang close by; otherwise it will go badly with you."

Then the fox stretched out his tail, and the king's son seated himself upon it, and away they went over stock and stone until the wind whistled through their hair. And everything happened just as the fox had said, and he came to the stall where the golden horse was: and as he was about to put on him the plain saddle, he thought to himself, "Such a beautiful animal would be disgraced were I not to put on him the good saddle, which becomes him so well." However, no sooner did the horse feel the golden saddle touch him than he began to neigh. And the grooms all awoke, seized the king's son and threw him into prison. The next morning he was delivered up to justice and condemned to death, but the king promised him his life, and also to bestow upon him the golden horse, if he could convey thither the beautiful princess of the golden castle.

With a heavy heart the king's son set out, but by great good luck he soon met with the faithful fox.

"I ought now to leave you to your own ill-luck," said the fox, "but I am sorry for you, and will once more help you in your need. Your way lies straight up to the golden castle: you will arrive there in the evening, and at night, when all is quiet, the beautiful princess goes to the bath. And as she is entering the bathing-house, go up to her and give her a kiss, then she will follow you, and you can lead her away; but do not suffer her first to go and take leave of her parents, or it will go ill with you."

Then the fox stretched out his tail; the king's son seated himself upon it, and away they went over stock and stone, so that the wind whistled through their hair. And when he came to the golden castle all was as the fox had said. He waited until midnight, when all lay in deep sleep, and then as the beautiful princess went to the bathing-house he went up to her and gave her a kiss, and she willingly promised to go with him, but she begged him earnestly, and with tears, that he would let her first go and take leave of her parents. At first he denied her prayer, but as she wept so much the more, and fell at his feet, he gave in at last. And no sooner had the princess reached her father's bedside than he, and all who were in the castle, woke up, and the young man was seized and thrown into prison.

The next morning the king said to him, "Thy life is forfeit, but thou shalt find grace if thou canst level that mountain that lies before my windows, and over which I am not able to see: and if this is done within eight days thou shalt have my daughter for a reward."

So the king's son set to work, and dug and shovelled away without ceasing, but when, on the seventh day, he saw how little he had accomplished, and that all his work was as nothing, he fell into great sadness, and gave up all hope. But on the evening of the seventh day the fox appeared, and said, "You do not deserve that I should help you, but go now and lie down to sleep, and I will do the work for you."

The next morning when he awoke, and looked out of the window, the mountain had disappeared. The young man hastened full of joy to the king, and told him that his behest was fulfilled, and, whether the king liked it or not, he had to keep to his word, and let his daughter go.

So they both went away together, and it

was not long before the faithful fox came up to them.

"Well, you have got the best first," said he; "but you must know the golden horse belongs to the princess of the golden castle."

"But how shall I get it?" asked the young man.

"I am going to tell you," answered the fox. "First, go to the king who sent you to the golden castle, and take to him the beautiful princess. There will then be very great rejoicing; he will willingly give you the golden horse, and they will lead him out to you; then mount him without delay, and stretch out your hand to each of them to take leave, and last of all to the princess, and when you have her by the hand swing her up on the horse behind you, and off you go! nobody will be able to overtake you, for that horse goes swifter than the wind."

And so it was all happily done, and the king's son carried off the beautiful princess on the golden horse. The fox did not stay behind, and he said to the young man, "Now, I will help you to get the golden bird. When you draw near the castle where the bird is, let the lady alight, and I will take her under my care; then you must ride the golden horse into the castle-yard, and there will be great rejoicing to see it, and they will bring out to you the golden bird; as soon as you have the cage in your hand, you must start off back to us, and then you shall carry the lady away."

The plan was successfully carried out; and when the young man returned with the treasure, the fox said, "Now, what will you give me for my reward?"

"What would you like?" asked the young man.

"When we are passing through the wood, I desire that you should slay me, and cut my head and feet off."

"That were a strange sign of gratitude," said the king's son, "and I could not possibly do such a thing."

Then said the fox, "If you will not do it, I must leave you; but before I go let me give you some good advice. Beware of two things: buy no gallows-meat, and sit at no brook-side." With that the fox ran off into the wood.

The young man thought to himself, "That is a wonderful animal, with most singular ideas. How should any one buy gallows-meat? and I am sure I have no particular fancy for sitting by a brook-side."

So he rode on with the beautiful princess, and their way led them through the village where his two brothers had stayed. There they heard great outcry and noise, and when he asked what it was all about, they told him that two people were going to be hanged. And when he drew near he saw that it was his two brothers, who had done all sorts of evil tricks, and had wasted all their goods. He asked if there were no means of setting them free.

"Oh yes! if you will buy them off,"
answered the people; "but why should you
spend your money in redeeming such
worthless men?"

But he persisted in doing so; and when
they were let go they all went on their journey together.

After a while they came to the wood
where the fox had met them first, and there
it seemed so cool and sheltered from the
sun's burning rays that the two brothers said,
"Let us rest here for a little by the brook, and
eat and drink to refresh ourselves."

The young man consented, quite forgetting the fox's warning, and he seated himself
by the brook-side, suspecting no evil. But
the two brothers thrust him backwards into
the brook, seized the princess, the horse,
and the bird, and went home to their father.

"Is not this the golden bird that we bring?"
said they; "and we have also the golden
horse, and the princess of the golden castle."

Then there was great rejoicing in the royal
castle, but the horse did not feed, the bird
did not chirp, and the princess sat still and
wept.

The youngest brother, however, had not
perished. The brook was, by good fortune,
dry, and he fell on soft moss without receiv-
ing any hurt, but he could not get up again.
But in his need the faithful fox was not
lacking; he came up running, and reproached
him for having forgotten his advice.

"But I cannot forsake you all the same," said he; "I will help you back again into daylight." So he told the young man to grasp his tail, and hold on to it fast, and so he drew him up again.

"Still you are not quite out of all danger," said the fox; "your brothers, not being certain of your death, have surrounded the wood with sentinels, who are to put you to death if you let yourself be seen."

A poor beggar-man was sitting by the path, and the young man changed clothes with him, and went clad in that wise into the king's courtyard. Nobody knew him, but the bird began to chirp, and the horse began to feed, and the beautiful princess ceased weeping.

"What does this mean?" said the king, astonished.

The princess answered, "I cannot tell, except that I was sad, and now I am joyful; it is to me as if my rightful bridegroom had returned."

Then she told him all that happened, although the two brothers had threatened to put her to death if she let out anything. The king then ordered every person who was in the castle to be brought before him, and with the rest came the young man like a beggar in his wretched garments; but the princess knew him, and greeted him well, falling on his neck and kissing him. The wicked brothers were seized and put to death, and the youngest brother was married to the princess, and succeeded to the inheritance of his father.

But what became of the poor fox? Long afterwards the king's son was going through the wood, and the fox met him and said, "Now, you have everything that you can wish for, but my misfortunes never come to an end, and it lies in your power to free me from them." And once more he prayed the king's son earnestly to slay him, and cut off his head and feet. So, at last, he consented, and no sooner was it done than the fox was changed into a man, and was no other than the brother of the beautiful princess; and thus he was set free from a spell that had bound him for a long, long time.

And now, indeed, there lacked nothing to their happiness as long as they lived.

There was a man who had three sons, the youngest of whom was called the Simpleton, and was despised, laughed at, and neglected, on every occasion. It happened one day that the eldest son wished to go into the forest to cut wood, and before he went his mother gave him a delicious pancake and a flask of wine, that he might not suffer from hunger or thirst. When he came into the forest a little old grey man met him, who wished him good day, and said, "Give me a bit of cake out of your pocket, and let me have a drink of your wine; I am so hungry and thirsty."

But the prudent youth answered, "Give you my cake and my wine? I haven't got any; be off with you."

And leaving the little man standing there, he went off. Then he began to fell a tree, but he had not been at it long before he made a wrong stroke, and the hatchet hit him in the arm, so that he was obliged to go home and get it bound up. That was what came of the little grey man.

Afterwards the second son went into the

wood, and the mother gave to him, as to the eldest, a pancake and a flask of wine. The little old grey man met him also, and begged for a little bit of cake and a drink of wine. But the second son spoke out plainly, saying, "What I give you I lose myself, so be off with you."

And leaving the little man standing there, he went off. The punishment followed; as he was chopping away at the tree, he hit himself in the leg so severely that he had to be carried home.

Then said the Simpleton, "Father, let me go for once into the forest to cut wood"; and the father answered, "Your brothers have hurt themselves by so doing; give it up, you understand nothing about it."

But the Simpleton went on begging so long, that the father said at last, "Well, be off with you; you will only learn by experience."

The mother gave him a cake (it was only made with water, and baked in the ashes), and with it a flask of sour beer. When he came into the forest the little old grey man met him, and greeted him, saying, "Give me a bit of your cake, and a drink from your flask; I am so hungry and thirsty."

And the Simpleton answered, "I have only a flour and water cake and sour beer; but if that is good enough for you, let us sit down together and eat." Then they sat down, and as the Simpleton took out his flour and water cake it became a rich pancake, and his sour beer became good wine; then they ate and drank, and afterwards the little man said, "As you have such a kind heart, and share what you have so willingly, I will bestow good luck upon you. Yonder stands an old tree; cut it down, and at its roots you will find something," and thereupon the little man took his departure.

The Simpleton went there, and hewed away at the tree, and when it fell he saw, sitting among the roots, a goose with feathers of pure gold. He lifted it out and took it with him to an inn where he intended to stay the night. The landlord had three daughters who, when they saw the goose, were curious to know what wonderful kind of bird it was, and ended by longing for one of its golden feathers. The eldest thought, "I will wait for a good opportunity, and then I will pull out one of its feathers for myself;" and so, when the Simpleton was gone out, she seized the goose by its wing—but there her finger and hand had to stay, held fast. Soon after came the second sister with the same idea of plucking out one of the golden feathers for herself; but scarcely had she touched her sister, than she also was obliged to stay, held fast. Lastly came the third with the same intentions; but the others screamed out, "Stay away! for heaven's sake stay away!"

But she did not see why she should stay away, and thought, "If they do so, why should not I?" and went towards them. But when she reached her sisters there she stopped, hanging on with them. And so they had to stay, all night. The next morning the Simpleton took the goose under his arm and went away, unmindful of the three girls that hung on to it. The three had always to run after him, left and right, wherever his legs carried him. In the midst of the fields they met the parson, who, when he saw the procession, said, "Shame on you, girls, running after a young fellow through the fields like this," and forthwith he seized hold of the youngest by the hand to drag her away, but hardly had he touched her when he too was obliged to run after them himself. Not long after the sexton came that way, and seeing the respected parson following at the heels of the three girls, he called out, "Ho, your reverence, whither away so quickly? You forget that we have another christening today;" and he seized hold of him by his gown; but no sooner had he touched him than he was obliged to follow on too. As the five tramped on, one after another, two peasants with their hoes came up from the fields, and the parson cried out to them, and begged them to come and set him and the sexton free, but no sooner had they touched the sexton than they had to follow on too; and now there were seven following the Simpleton and the goose.

By and by they came to a town where a king reigned, who had an only daughter who was so serious that no one could make her laugh; therefore the king had given out that whoever should make her laugh should have her in marriage. The Simpleton, when he heard this, went with his goose and his hangers-on into the presence of the king's daughter, and as soon as she saw the seven people following always one after the other, she burst out laughing, and seemed as if she could never stop. And so the Simpleton earned a right to her as his bride; but the king did not like him for a son-in-law and made all kinds of objections, and said he must first bring a man who could drink up a whole cellar of wine. The Simpleton thought that the little grey man would be able to help him, and went out into the forest, and there, on the very spot where he felled the tree, he saw a man sitting with a very sad countenance. The Simpleton asked him what was the matter, and he answered, "I have a great thirst, which I cannot quench: cold water does not agree with me; I have indeed drunk up a whole cask of wine, but what good is a drop like that?"

Then said the Simpleton, "I can help you; only come with me, and you shall have enough."

He took him straight to the king's cellar, and the man sat himself down before the big vats, and drank, and drank, and before a day was over he had drunk up the whole cellar-full. The Simpleton again asked for his bride, but the king was annoyed that a wretched fellow, called the Simpleton by everybody, should carry off his daughter, and so he made new conditions. He was to produce a man who could eat up a mountain of bread. The Simpleton did not hesitate long, but ran quickly off to the forest, and there in the same place sat a man who had fastened a strap round his body, making a very piteous face, and saying, "I have eaten a whole bakehouse full of rolls, but what is the use of that when one is so hungry as I am? My stomach feels quite empty, and I am obliged to strap myself together, that I may not die of hunger."

The Simpleton was quite glad of this, and said, "Get up quickly, and come along with me, and you shall have enough to eat."

He led him straight to the king's court-yard, where all the meal in the kingdom had been collected and baked into a mountain of bread. The man out of the forest settled himself down before it and hastened to eat, and in one day the whole mountain had disappeared.

Then the Simpleton asked for his bride the third time. The king, however, found one more excuse, and said he must have a ship that should be able to sail on land or on water.

"So soon," said he, "as you come sailing along with it, you shall have my daughter for your wife."

. . . the ship that could sail on land and on water, . . . (page 241)

The Simpleton went straight to the forest, and there sat the little old grey man with whom he had shared his cake, and he said, "I have eaten for you, and I have drunk for you, I will also give you the ship; and all because you were kind to me at the first."

Then he gave him the ship that could sail on land and on water, and when the king saw it he knew he could no longer withhold his daughter. The marriage took place immediately, and at the death of the king the Simpleton possessed the kingdom, and lived long and happily with his wife.

There was a certain village where lived many rich farmers and only one poor one, whom they called the Little Farmer. He had not even a cow, and still less had he money to buy one; and he and his wife greatly wished for such a thing. One day he said to her, "Listen, I have a good idea; it is that your godfather the joiner shall make us a calf of wood and paint it brown, so as to look just like any other; and then in time perhaps it will grow big and become a cow."

This notion pleased the wife, and godfather joiner set to work to saw and plane, and soon turned out a calf complete, with its head down and neck stretched out as if it were grazing.

The next morning, as the cows were driven to pasture, the Little Farmer called out to the drover, "Look here, I have got a little calf to go, but it is still young and must be carried."

"All right!" said the drover, and tucked it under his arm, carried it into the meadows, and stood it in the grass. So the calf stayed where it was put, and seemed to be eating all the time, and the drover thought to himself, "It will soon be able to run alone, if it grazes at that rate!"

In the evening, when the herds had to be driven home, he said to the calf, "If you can stand there eating like that, you can just walk off on your own four legs; I am not going to lug you under my arm again!"

But the Little Farmer was standing by his house door, and waiting for his calf; and when he saw the cow-herd coming through the village without it, he asked what it meant. The cow-herd answered, "It is still out there eating away, and never attended to the call, and would not come with the rest."

Then the Little Farmer said, "I will tell you what, I must have my beast brought home."

And they went together through the fields in quest of it, but some one had stolen it, and it was gone. And the drover said, "Most likely it has run away."

But the Little Farmer said "Not it!" and brought the cow-herd before the bailiff, who ordered him for his carelessness to give the Little Farmer a cow for the missing calf.

So now the Little Farmer and his wife possessed their long-wished-for cow; they rejoiced with all their hearts, but unfortunately they had no fodder for it, and could give it nothing to eat, so that before long they had to kill it. Its flesh they salted down, and the Little Farmer went to the town to sell the skin and buy a new calf with what he got for it. On the way he came to a mill, where a raven was sitting with broken wings, and he took it up out of pity and wrapped it in the skin. The weather was very stormy, and it blew and rained, so he turned into the mill and asked for shelter. The miller's wife was alone in the house, and she said to the Little Farmer, "Well, come in and lay thee down in the straw," and she gave him a piece of bread and cheese. So the Little Farmer ate, and then lay down with his skin near him, and the miller's wife thought he was sleeping with fatigue. After a while in came another man, and the miller's wife received him very well, saying, "My husband is out; we will make good cheer."

The Little Farmer listened to what they said, and when he heard good cheer spoken of, he grew angry to think he had been put off with bread and cheese. For the miller's wife presently brought out roast meat, salad, cakes, and wine.

Now as the pair were sitting down to their feast, there came a knock at the door.

"Oh dear," cried the woman, "it is my husband!" In a twinkling she popped the roast meat into the oven, the wine under the pillow, the salad in the bed, the cakes under the bed, and the man in the linen closet. Then she opened the door to her husband, saying, "Thank goodness you are here! what weather it is, as if the world were coming to an end!"

When the miller saw the Little Farmer lying in the straw, he said, "What fellow have you got there?"

"Oh!" said the wife, "the poor chap came in the midst of the wind and rain and asked for shelter, and I gave him some bread and cheese and spread some straw for him."

The husband answered, "Oh well, I have no objection, only get me something to eat at once."

But the wife said, "There is nothing but bread and cheese."

"Anything will do for me," answered the miller, "bread and cheese for ever!" and catching sight of the Little Farmer, he cried, "Come along, and keep me company!" The Little Farmer did not wait to be asked twice, but sat down and ate. After a while the miller noticed the skin lying on the ground with the raven wrapped up in it, and he said, "What have you got there?"

The Little Farmer answered, "A fortune-teller."

And the miller asked "Can he tell my fortune?"

"Why not?" answered the Little Farmer. "He will tell four things, and the fifth he keeps to himself." Now the miller became very curious, and said, "Ask him to say something."

And the Little Farmer pinched the raven, so that it croaked, "Crr, crr." "What does he say?" asked the miller. And the Little Farmer answered, "First he says that there is wine under the pillow."

"That would be jolly!" cried the miller, and he went to look, and found the wine, and then asked, "What next?"

So the Little Farmer made the raven croak again, and then said, "He says, secondly, that there is roast meat in the oven."

"That would be jolly!" cried the miller, and he went and looked, and found the roast meat. The Little Farmer made the fortune-teller speak again, and then said, "He says, thirdly, that there is salad in the bed."

"That would be jolly!" cried the miller, and went and looked, and found the salad. Once more the Little Farmer pinched the raven, so that he croaked, and said, "He says, fourthly and lastly, that there are cakes under the bed."

"That would be jolly!" cried the miller,

and he went and looked, and found the cakes.

And now the two sat down to table, and the miller's wife felt very uncomfortable, and she went to bed and took all the keys with her. The miller was eager to know what the fifth thing could be, but the Little Farmer said, "Suppose we eat the four things in peace first, for the fifth thing is a great deal worse."

So they sat and ate, and while they ate, they bargained together as to how much the miller would give for knowing the fifth thing; and at last they agreed upon three hundred dollars. Then the Little Farmer pinched the raven, so that he croaked aloud. And the miller asked what he said, and the Little Farmer answered, "He says that there is a demon in the linen-closet."

"Then," said the miller, "that demon must out of the linen-closet," and he unbarred the house-door, while the Little Farmer got the key of the linen-closet from the miller's wife, and opened it. Then the man rushed forth, and out of the house, and the miller said, "I saw the black rogue with my own eyes; so that is a good riddance."

And the Little Farmer took himself off by daybreak next morning with the three hundred dollars.

And after this the Little Farmer by degrees got on in the world, and built himself a good house, and the other farmers said, "Surely the Little Farmer has been where it rains gold pieces, and has brought home money by the bushel."

And he was summoned before the bailiff to say whence his riches came. And all he said was, "I sold my calf's skin for three hundred dollars."

When the other farmers heard this they wished to share such good luck, and ran home, killed all their cows, skinned them in order to sell them also for the same high price as the Little Farmer. And the bailiff said, "I must be beforehand with them." So he sent his servant into the town to the skin buyer, and he only gave her three dollars for the skin, and that was faring better than the others, for when they came, they did not get as much as that, for the skin buyer said, "What am I to do with all these skins?"

Now the other farmers were very angry with the Little Farmer for misleading them, and they vowed vengeance against him, and went to complain of his deceit to the bailiff. The poor Little Farmer was with one voice sentenced to death, and to be put into a cask with holes in it, and rolled into the water. So he was led to execution, and a priest was fetched to say a mass for him, and the rest of the people had to stand at a distance. As soon as the Little Farmer caught sight of the priest he knew him for the man who was hid in the linen-closet at the miller's. And he said to him, "As I let you out of the cupboard, you must let me out of the cask."

At that moment a shepherd passed with a flock of sheep, and the Little Farmer knowing him to have a great wish to become bailiff himself, called out with all his might, "No, I will not, and if all the world asked me, I would not!"

The shepherd, hearing him, came up and asked what it was he would not do. The Little Farmer answered, "They want to make me bailiff, if I sit in this cask, but I will not do it!"

The shepherd said, "If that is all there is to do in order to become bailiff I will sit in the cask and welcome." And the Little Farmer answered, "Yes, that is all, just you get into the cask, and you will become bailiff." So the shepherd agreed, and got in, and the Little Farmer fastened on the top; then he collected the herd of sheep and drove them away. The priest went back to the parish-assembly, and told them the mass had been said. Then they came and began to roll the cask into the water, and as it went the shepherd inside called out, "I consent to be bailiff!"

They thought that it was the Little Farmer who spoke, and they answered, "All right; but first you must go down below and look about you a little," and they rolled the cask into the water.

Upon that the farmers went home, and when they reached the village, there they met the Little Farmer driving a flock of sheep, and looking quite calm and contented. The farmers were astonished and cried, "Little Farmer, whence come you? how did you get out of the water?"

"Oh, easily," answered he, "I sank and sank until I came to the bottom; then I broke through the cask and came out of it, and there were beautiful meadows and plenty of sheep feeding, so I brought away this flock with me."

Then said the farmers, "Are there any left?"

"Oh yes," answered the Little Farmer, "more than you can possibly need."

Then the farmers agreed that they would go and fetch some sheep also, each man a flock for himself; and the bailiff said, "Me first." And they all went together, and in the blue sky there were little fleecy clouds like lambkins, and they were reflected in the water; and the farmers cried out, "There are the sheep down there at the bottom."

When the bailiff heard that he pressed forward and said, "I will go first and look about me, and if things look well, I will call to you."

And he jumped into the water, and they all thought that the noise he made meant "Come," so the whole company jumped in one after the other. So perished all the proprietors of the village, and the Little Farmer, as sole heir, became a rich man.

s a merry young huntsman was once going briskly along through a wood, there came up a little old woman, and said to him, "Good day, good day; you seem merry enough, but I am hungry and thirsty; do pray give me something to eat." The huntsman took pity on her, and put his hand in his pocket and gave her what he had. Then he wanted to go his way; but she took hold of him, and said, "Listen, my friend, to what I am going to tell you; I will reward you for your kindness; go your way, and after a little time you will come to a tree where you will see nine birds sitting on a cloak. Shoot into the midst of them, and one will fall down dead: the cloak will fall too; take it, it is a wishing-cloak, and when you wear it you will find yourself at any place where you may wish to be. Cut open the dead bird, take out its heart and keep it, and you will find a piece of gold under your pillow every morning when you rise. It is the bird's heart that will bring you this good luck."

The huntsman thanked her, and thought to himself. "If all this does happen, it will be a

fine thing for me." When he had gone a hundred steps or so, he heard a screaming and chirping in the branches over him, and looked up and saw a flock of birds pulling a cloak with their bills and feet; screaming, fighting, and tugging at each other as if each wished to have it himself. "Well," said the huntsman, "this is wonderful; this happens just as the old woman said;" then he shot into the midst of them so that their feathers flew all about. Off went the flock chattering away; but one fell down dead, and the cloak with it. Then the huntsman did as the old woman told him, cut open the bird, took out the heart, and carried the cloak home with him.

The next morning when he awoke he lifted up his pillow, and there lay the piece of gold glittering underneath; the same happened next day, and indeed every day when he arose. He heaped up a great deal of gold, and at last thought to himself. "Of what use is this gold to me whilst I am at home? I will go out into the world and look about me."

Then he took leave of his friends, and hung his bag and bow about his neck, and went his way. It so happened that his road one day led through a thick wood, at the end of which was a large castle in a green meadow, and at one of the windows stood an old woman with a very beautiful young lady by her side looking about them. Now the old woman was a fairy, and said to the young lady, "There is a young man coming out of the wood who carries a wonderful prize; we must get it away from him, my dear child, for it is more fit for us than for him. He has a bird's heart that brings a piece of gold under his pillow every morning." Meantime the huntsman came nearer and looked at the lady, and said to himself, "I have been travelling so long that I should like to go into this castle and rest myself, for I have money enough to pay for any thing I want;" but the real reason was, that he wanted to see more of the beautiful lady. Then he went into the house, and was welcomed kindly; and it was not long before he was so much in love that he thought of nothing else but looking at the lady's eyes, and doing every thing that she wished. Then the old woman said, "Now is the time for getting the bird's heart." So the lady stole it away, and he never found any more gold under his pillow, for it lay now under the young lady's, and the old woman took it away every morning; but he was so much in love that he never missed his prize.

"Well," said the old fairy, "we have got the bird's heart, but not the wishing-cloak yet, and that we must also get." "Let us leave him that," said the young lady; "he has already lost his wealth." Then the fairy was very angry, and said, "Such a cloak is a very rare and wonderful thing, and I must and will have it." So she did as the old woman told her, and set herself at the window, and looked about the country and seemed very sorrowful; then the huntsman said, "What makes you so sad?" "Alas! dear sir," said she, "yonder lies the granite rock where all the costly diamonds grow, and I want so much to go there, that whenever I think of it I cannot help being sorrowful, for who can reach it? only the birds and the flies—man cannot." "If that's all your grief," said the huntsman, "I'll take you there with all my heart;" so he drew her under his cloak, and the moment he wished to be on the granite mountain they were both there. The diamonds glittered so on all sides that they were delighted with the sight and picked up the finest. But the old fairy made a deep sleep come upon him, and he said to the young lady, "Let us sit down and rest ourselves a little, I am so tired that I cannot stand any longer." So they sat down, and he laid his head in her lap and fell asleep; and whilst he was sleeping on she took the cloak from his shoulders, hung it on her own, picked up the diamonds, and wished herself home again.

When he awoke and found that his lady had tricked him, and left him alone on the wild rock, he said, "Alas! what roguery there is in the world!" and there he sat in great grief and fear, not knowing what to do. Now this rock belonged to fierce giants who lived upon it; and as he saw three of them striding about, he thought to himself, "I can only save myself by feigning to be asleep;" so he laid himself down as if he were in a sound sleep. When the giants came up to him, the first pushed him with his foot, and said, "What worm is this that lies here curled up?" "Tread upon him and kill him," said the second. "It's not worth the trouble," said the third; "let him live, he'll go climbing higher up the mountain, and some cloud will come rolling and carry him away." And they passed on. But the huntsman had heard all they said; and as soon as they were gone, he climbed to the top of the mountain, and when he had sat there a short time a cloud came rolling around him, and caught him in a whirlwind and bore him along for some time, till it settled in a garden, and he fell quite gently to the ground amongst the greens and cabbages.

Then he looked around him, and said, "I wish I had something to eat, if not I shall be worse off than before; for here I see neither apples nor pears, nor any kind of fruits, nothing but vegetables." At last he thought to himself, "I can eat salad, it will refresh and strengthen me." So he picked out a fine head and ate of it; but scarcely had he swallowed two bites when he felt himself quite changed, and saw with horror that he was turned into an ass. However, he still felt very hungry, and the salad tasted very nice; so he ate on till he came to another kind of salad, and scarcely had he tasted it when he felt another change come over him, and soon saw that he was lucky enough to have found his old shape again.

Then he laid himself down and slept off a little of his weariness; and when he awoke the next morning he broke off a head both of the good and the bad salad, and thought to himself, "This will help me to my fortune again, and enable me to pay off some folks for their treachery." So he went away to try and find the castle of his old friends; and after wandering about a few days he luckily found it. Then he stained his face all over brown, so that even his mother would not have known him, and went into the castle and asked for a lodging; "I am so tired," said he, "that I can go no farther." "Countryman," said the fairy, "who are you? and what is your business?" "I am," said he, "a messenger sent by the king to find the finest salad that grows under the sun. I have been lucky enough to find it, and have brought it with me; but the heat of the sun scorches so that it begins to wither, and I don't know that I can carry it farther."

When the fairy and the young lady heard of this beautiful salad, they longed to taste it, and said, "Dear countryman, let us just taste it." "To be sure," answered he; "I have two heads of it with me, and will give you one;" so he opened his bag and gave them the bad. Then the fairy herself took it into the kitchen to be dressed; and when it was ready she could not wait till it was carried up, but took a few leaves immediately and put them in her mouth, and scarcely were they swallowed when she lost her own form and ran braying down into the court in the form of an ass. Now the servant maid came into the kitchen, and seeing the salad ready, was going to carry it up; but on the way she too felt a wish to taste it as the old woman had done, and ate some leaves; so she also was turned into an ass and ran after the other, letting the dish with the salad fall on the ground. The messenger sat all this time with the beautiful young lady, and as nobody came with the salad and she longed to taste it, she said, "I don't know where the salad can be." Then he thought something must have happened, and said, "I will go into the kitchen and see." And as he went he saw two asses in the court running about, and the salad lying on the ground. "All right!" said he; "those two have had their share." Then he took up the rest of the leaves, laid them on the dish and brought them to the young lady, saying, "I bring you the dish myself that you may not wait any longer." So she ate of it, and like the others ran off into the court, braying away.

Then the huntsman washed his face and went into the court that they might know him. "Now you shall be paid for your roguery," said he; and tied them all three to a rope and took them along with him till he came to a mill and knocked at the window. "What's the matter?" said the miller. "I have three tiresome beasts here," and the other; "if you will take them, give them food and room, and treat them as I tell you, I will pay you whatever you ask." "With all my heart," said the miller; "but how shall I treat them?" Then the huntsman said, "Give the old one stripes three times a day and hay once; give the next (who was the servant-maid) stripes once a day and hay three times; and give the youngest (who was the beautiful lady) hay three times a day and no stripes;" for he could not find it in his heart to have her beaten. After this he went back to the castle, where he found every thing he wanted.

Some days after the miller came to him and told him that the old ass was dead; "the other two," said he, "are alive and eat, but are so sorrowful that they cannot last long." Then the huntsman pitied them, and told the miller to drive them back to him, and when they came, he gave them some of the good salad to eat. And the beautiful young lady fell upon her knees before him, and said, "O dearest huntsman! forgive me all the ill I have done you; my mother forced me to it, it was against my will, for I always loved you very much. Your wishing-cloak hangs up in the closet, and as for the bird's heart, I will give it you too." But he said, "Keep it, it will be just the same thing, for I mean to make you my wife." So they were married, and lived together very happily till they died.

here was once a rich man whose wife lay sick, and when she felt her end drawing near she called to her only daughter to come near her bed, and said, "Dear child, be pious and good, and God will always take care of you, and I will look down upon you from heaven, and will be with you."

And then she closed her eyes and expired. The maiden went every day to her mother's grave and wept, and was always pious and good. When the winter came the snow covered the grave with a white covering, and when the sun came in the early spring and melted it away, the man took to himself another wife.

The new wife brought two daughters home with her, and they were beautiful and fair in appearance, but at heart were black and ugly. And then began very evil times for the poor step-daughter.

"Is the stupid creature to sit in the same room with us?" said they; "those who eat food must earn it. Out upon her for a kitchen-maid!"

They took away her pretty dresses, and

put on her an old grey kirtle, and gave her wooden shoes to wear.

"Just look now at the proud princess, how she is decked out!" cried they laughing, and then they sent her into the kitchen. There she was obliged to do heavy work from morning to night, get up early in the morning, draw water, make the fires, cook, and wash. Besides that, the sisters did their utmost to torment her,—mocking her, and strewing peas and lentils among the ashes, and setting her to pick them up. In the evenings, when she was quite tired out with her hard day's work, she had no bed to lie on, but was obliged to rest on the hearth among the cinders. And as she always looked dusty and dirty, they named her Aschenputtel.

It happened one day that the father went to the fair, and he asked his two step-daughters what he should bring back for them.

"Fine clothes!" said one.

"Pearls and jewels!" said the other.

"But what will you have, Aschenputtel?" said he.

"The first twig, father, that strikes against your hat on the way home; that is what I should like you to bring me."

So he bought for the two step-daughters fine clothes, pearls, and jewels, and on his way back, as he rode through a green lane, a hazel-twig struck against his hat; and he broke it off and carried it home with him. And when he reached home he gave to the step-daughters what they had wished for, and to Aschenputtel he gave the hazel-twig. She thanked him, and went to her mother's grave, and planted this twig there, weeping so bitterly that the tears fell upon it and watered it, and it flourished and became a fine tree. Aschenputtel went to see it three times a day, and wept and prayed, and each time a white bird rose up from the tree, and if she uttered any wish the bird brought her whatever she had wished for.

Now it came to pass that the king ordained a festival that should last for three days, and to which all the beautiful young women of that country were bidden, so that the king's son might choose a bride from among them. When the two step-daughters heard that they too were bidden to appear, they felt very pleased, and they called Aschenputtel, and said, "Comb our hair, brush our shoes, and make our buckles fast, we are going to the wedding feast at the king's castle."

Aschenputtel, when she heard this, could not help crying, for she too would have liked to go to the dance, and she begged her step-mother to allow her.

"What, you Aschenputtel!" said she, "in all your dust and dirt, you want to go to the festival! you that have no dress and no shoes! you want to dance!"

But as she persisted in asking, at last the step-mother said, "I have strewed a dish-full of lentils in the ashes, and if you can pick them all up again in two hours you may go with us."

Then the maiden went to the back-door that led into the garden, and called out,

> "O gentle doves, O turtle-doves,
> And all the birds that be,
> The lentils that in ashes lie
> Come and pick up for me!
> The good must be put in the dish,
> The bad you may eat if you wish."

Then there came to the kitchen-window two white doves, and after them some turtle-doves, and at last a crowd of all the birds under heaven, chirping and fluttering, and they alighted among the ashes; and the doves nodded with their heads, and began to pick, peck, pick, peck, and then all the others began to pick, peck, pick, peck, and put all the good grains into the dish. Before an hour was over all was done, and they flew away. Then the maiden brought the dish to her step-mother, feeling joyful, and thinking that now she should go to the feast; but the step-mother said, "No, Aschenputtel, you have no proper clothes, and you do not know how to dance, and you would be laughed at!"

And when Aschenputtel cried for disappointment, she added, "If you can pick two dishes full of lentils out of the ashes, nice and clean, you shall go with us," thinking to herself, "for that is not possible." When she had strewed two dishes full of lentils among the ashes the maiden went through the back-door into the garden, and cried,

"O gentle doves, O turtle-doves,

The bad you may eat if you wish."

So there came to the kitchen-window two white doves, and then some turtle-doves, and at last a crowd of all the other birds under heaven, chirping and fluttering, and they alighted among the ashes, and the doves nodded with their heads and began to pick, peck, pick, peck, and then all the others began to pick, peck, pick, peck, and put all the good grains into the dish. And before half-an-hour was over it was all done, and they flew away. Then the maiden took the dishes to the step-mother, feeling joyful, and thinking that now she should go with them to the feast; but she said "All this is of no good to you; you cannot come with us, for you have no proper clothes, and cannot dance; you would put us to shame."

Then she turned her back on poor Aschenputtel, and made haste to set out with her two proud daughters.

And as there was no one left in the house, Aschenputtel went to her mother's grave, under the hazel bush, and cried,

. . . she ran past him so quickly that he could not follow her. (page 267)

Then the bird threw down a dress of gold and silver, and a pair of slippers embroidered with silk and silver. And in all haste she put on the dress and went to the festival. But her step-mother and sisters did not know her, and thought she must be a foreign princess, she looked so beautiful in her golden dress. Of Aschenputtel they never thought at all, and supposed that she was sitting at home, and picking the lentils out of the ashes. The king's son came to meet her, and took her by the hand and danced with her, and he refused to stand up with any one else, so that he might not be obliged to let go her hand; and when any one came to claim it he answered, "She is my partner."

And when the evening came she wanted to go home, but the prince said he would go with her to take care of her, for he wanted to see where the beautiful maiden lived. But she escaped him, and jumped up into the pigeon-house. Then the prince waited until the father came, and told him the strange maiden had jumped into the pigeon-house. The father thought to himself, "It cannot surely be Aschenputtel," and called for axes and hatchets, and had the pigeon-house cut down, but there was no one in it. And when they entered the house there sat Aschenputtel in her dirty clothes among the cinders, and a little oil-lamp burnt dimly in the chimney; for Aschenputtel had been very quick, and had jumped out of the pigeon-house again, and had run to the hazel bush; and there she had taken off her beautiful dress and had laid it on the grave, and the bird had carried it away again, and then she had put on her little grey kirtle again, and had sat down in the kitchen among the cinders.

The next day, when the festival began anew, and the parents and step-sisters had gone to it, Aschenputtel went to the hazel bush and cried,

"Little tree, little tree, shake over me,
That silver and gold may come down and cover me."

Then the bird cast down a still more splendid dress than on the day before. And when she appeared in it among the guests every one was astonished at her beauty. The prince had been waiting until she came, and he took her hand and danced with her alone. And when any one else came to invite her he said, "She is my partner."

And when the evening came she wanted to go home, and the prince followed her, for he wanted to see to what house she belonged; but she broke away from him, and ran into the garden at the back of the house. There stood a fine large tree, bearing splendid pears; she leapt as lightly as a squirrel among the branches, and the prince did not know what had become of her. So he waited until the father came, and then he told him that the strange maiden had rushed from him, and that he thought she had gone up into the pear-tree. The father thought to himself, "It cannot surely be Aschenputtel," and called for an axe, and felled the tree, but there was no one in it. And when they went into the kitchen there sat Aschenputtel among the cinders, as usual, for she had got down the other side of the tree, and had taken back her beautiful clothes to the bird on the hazel bush, and had put on her old grey kirtle again.

On the third day, when the parents and the step-children had set off, Aschenputtel went again to her mother's grave, and said to the tree,

"Little tree, little tree, shake over me,
That silver and gold may come down and cover me."

Then the bird cast down a dress, the like of which had never been seen for splendor and brilliancy, and slippers that were of gold. And when she appeared in this dress at the feast nobody knew what to say for wonderment. The prince danced with her alone, and if any one else asked her he answered, "She is my partner."

And when it was evening Aschenputtel wanted to go home, and the prince was about to go with her, when she ran past him so quickly that he could not follow her. But he had laid a plan, and had caused all the steps to be spread with pitch, so that as she rushed down them the left shoe of the maiden remained sticking in it. The prince picked it up, and saw that it was of gold, and very small and slender. The next morning he went to the father and told him that none should be his bride save the one whose foot the golden shoe should fit. Then the two sisters were very glad, because they had pretty feet. The eldest went to her room to try on the shoe, and her mother stood by. But she could not get her great toe into it, for the shoe was too small; then her mother handed her a knife, and said, "Cut the toe off, for when you are queen you will never have to go on foot." So the girl cut her toe off, squeezed her foot into the shoe, concealed the pain, and went down to the prince. Then he took her with him on his horse as his bride, and rode off. They had to pass by the grave, and there sat the two pigeons on the hazel bush, and cried,

"There they go, there they go!
There is blood on her shoe;
The shoe is too small,
—Not the right bride at all!"

Then the prince looked at her shoe, and saw the blood flowing. And he turned his horse round and took the false bride home again, saying she was not the right one, and that the other sister must try on the shoe. So she went into her room to do so, and got her toes comfortably in, but her heel was too large. Then her mother handed her the knife, saying, "Cut a piece off your heel;

when you are queen you will never have to go on foot."

So the girl cut a piece off her heel, and thrust her foot into the shoe, concealed the pain, and went down to the prince, who took his bride before him on his horse and rode off. When they passed by the hazel bush the two pigeons sat there and cried,

"There they go, there they go!
There is blood on her shoe;
The shoe is too small,
—Not the right bride at all!"

Then the prince looked at her foot, and saw how the blood was flowing from the shoe, and staining the white stocking. And he turned his horse round and brought the false bride home again.

"This is not the right one," said he, "have you no other daughter?"

"No," said the man, "only my dead wife left behind her a little stunted Aschenputtel; it is impossible that she can be the bride." But the king's son ordered her to be sent for, but the mother said, "Oh no! she is much too dirty, I could not let her be seen."

But he would have her fetched, and so Aschenputtel had to appear.

First she washed her face and hands quite clean, and went in and curtseyed to the prince, who held out to her the golden shoe. Then she sat down on a stool, drew her foot out of the heavy wooden shoe, and slipped it into the golden one, which fitted it perfectly. And when she stood up, and the prince looked in her face, he knew again the beautiful maiden that had danced with him, and he cried, "This is the right bride!"

The step-mother and the two sisters were thunderstruck, and grew pale with anger; but he put Aschenputtel before him on his horse and rode off. And as they passed the hazel bush, the two white pigeons cried,

> "There they go, there they go!
> No blood on her shoe;
> The shoe's not too small,
> The right bride is she after all."

And when they had thus cried, they came flying after and perched on Aschenputtel's shoulders, one on the right, the other on the left, and so remained.

And when her wedding with the prince was appointed to be held, the false sisters came, hoping to curry favor, and to take part in the festivities. So as the bridal procession went to the church, the eldest walked on the right side and the younger on the left, and the pigeons picked out an eye of each of them. And as they returned the elder was on the left side and the younger on the right, and the pigeons picked out the other eye of each of them. And so they were condemned to go blind for the rest of their days because of their wickedness and falsehood.

here was once a fisherman and his wife who lived to-gether in a hovel by the sea-shore, and the fisherman went out every day with his hook and line to catch fish, and he angled and angled.

One day he was sitting with his rod and looking into the clear water, and he sat and sat.

At last down went the line to the bottom of the water, and when he drew it up he found a great flounder on the hook. And the flounder said to him, "Fisherman, listen to me; let me go, I am not a real fish but an enchanted prince. What good shall I be to you if you land me? I shall not taste well; so put me back into the water again, and let me swim away."

"Well," said the fisherman, "no need of so many words about the matter, as you can speak I had much rather let you swim away."

Then he put him back into the clear water, and the flounder sank to the bottom, leaving a long streak of blood behind him. Then the fisherman got up and went home to his wife in their hovel.

"Well, husband," said the wife, "have you caught nothing today?"

"No," said the man—"that is, I did catch a flounder, but as he said he was an enchanted prince, I let him go again."

"Then, did you wish for nothing?" said the wife.

"No," said the man; "what should I wish for?"

"Oh dear!" said the wife; "and it is so dreadful always to live in this evil-smelling hovel; you might as well have wished for a little cottage; go again and call him; tell him we want a little cottage, I daresay he will give it us; go, and be quick."

And when he went back, the sea was green and yellow, and not nearly so clear. So he stood and said,

> "O man, O man!—if man you be,
> Or flounder, flounder, in the sea—
> Such a tiresome wife I've got,
> For she wants what I do not."

Then the flounder came swimming up, and said, "Now then, what does she want?"

"Oh," said the man, "you know when I caught you my wife says I ought to have wished for something. She does not want to live any longer in the hovel, and would rather have a cottage.

"Go home with you," said the flounder, "she has it already."

So the man went home, and found, instead of the hovel, a little cottage, and his wife was sitting on a bench before the door. And she took him by the hand, and said to him, "Come in and see if this is not a great improvement."

So they went in, and there was a little house-place and a beautiful little bedroom, a kitchen and larder, with all sorts of furniture, and iron and brass ware of the very best. And at the back was a little yard with fowls and ducks, and a little garden full of green vegetables and fruit.

"Look," said the wife, "is not that nice?"

"Yes," said the man, "if this can only last we shall be very well contented."

"We will see about that," said the wife. And after a meal they went to bed.

So all went well for a week or fortnight, when the wife said, "Look here, husband, the cottage is really too confined, and the yard and garden are so small; I think the flounder had better get us a larger house; I should like very much to live in a large stone castle; so go to your fish and he will send us a castle."

"O my dear wife," said the man, "the cottage is good enough; what do we want a castle for?"

"We want one," said the wife; "go along with you; the flounder can give us one."

"Now, wife," said the man, "the flounder gave us the cottage; I do not like to go to him again, he may be angry."

"Go along," said the wife, "he might just

as well give us it as not; do as I say!"

The man felt very reluctant and unwilling; and he said to himself, "It is not the right thing to do;" nevertheless he went.

So when he came to the seaside, the water was purple and dark blue and grey and thick, and not green and yellow as before. And he stood and said,

> "O man, O man!—if man you be,
> Or flounder, flounder, in the sea—
> Such a tiresome wife I've got,
> For she wants what I do not."

"Now then, what does she want?" said the flounder.

"Oh," said the man, half frightened, "she wants to live in a large stone castle."

"Go home with you, she is already standing before the door," said the flounder.

Then the man went home, as he supposed, but when he got there, there stood in the place of the cottage a great castle of stone, and his wife was standing on the steps, about to go in; so she took him by the hand, and said, "Let us enter."

With that he went in with her, and in the castle was a great hall with a marble pavement, and there were a great many servants, who led them through large doors, and the passages were decked with tapestry, and the rooms with golden chairs and tables, and crystal chandeliers hanging from the ceiling; and all the rooms had carpets. And the tables were covered with eatables and the best wine for any one who wanted them. And at the back of the house was a great stable-yard for horses and cattle, and carriages of the finest; besides, there was a splendid large garden, with the most beautiful flowers and fine fruit trees, and a pleasance full half a mile long, with deer and oxen and sheep, and everything that heart could wish for.

"There!" said the wife, "is not this beautiful?"

"Oh yes," said the man, "if it will only last we can live in this fine castle and be very well contented."

"We will see about that," said the wife, "in the meanwhile we will sleep upon it." With that they went to bed.

The next morning the wife was awake first, just at the break of day, and she looked out and saw from her bed the beautiful country lying all round. The man took no notice of it, so she poked him in the side with her elbow, and said, "Husband, get up and just look out of the window. Look, just think if we could be king over all this country. Just go to your fish and tell him we should like to be king."

"Now, wife," said the man, "what should we be kings for? I don't want to be king."

"Well," said the wife, "if you don't want to be king, I will be king."

"Now, wife," said the man, "what do you want to be king for? I could not ask him such a thing."

"Why not?" said the wife, "you must go directly all the same; I must be king."

So the man went, very much put out that his wife should want to be king.

"It is not the right thing to do—not at all the right thing," thought the man. He did not at all want to go, and yet he went all the same.

And when he came to the sea the water was quite dark grey, and rushed far inland, and had an ill smell. And he stood and said,

> *"O man, O man!—if man you be,*
> *Or flounder, flounder, in the sea—*
> *Such a tiresome wife I've got,*
> *For she wants what I do not."*

"Now then, what does she want?" said the fish.

"Oh dear!" said the man, "she wants to be king."

"Go home with you, she is so already," said the fish.

So the man went back, and as he came to the palace he saw it was very much larger, and had great towers and splendid gateways; the herald stood before the door, and a number of soldiers with kettle-drums and trumpets.

And when he came inside everything was of marble and gold, and there were many curtains with great golden tassels. Then he went through the doors of the saloon to where the great throne-room was, and there was his wife sitting upon a throne of gold and diamonds, and she had a great golden crown on, and the sceptre in her hand was of pure gold and jewels, and on each side stood six pages in a row, each one a head shorter than the other. So the man went up to her and said, "Well, wife, so now you are king!"

"Yes," said the wife, "now I am king."

So then he stood and looked at her, and when he had gazed at her for some time he said, "Well, wife, this is fine for you to be king! now there is nothing more to wish for."

"O husband!" said the wife, seeming quite restless, "I am tired of this already. Go to your fish and tell him that now I am king I must be emperor."

"Now, wife," said the man, "what do you want to be emperor for?"

"Husband," said she, "go and tell the fish I want to be emperor."

"Oh dear!" said the man, "he could not do it—I cannot ask him such a thing. There is but one emperor at a time; the fish can't possibly make any one emperor—indeed he can't."

"Now, look here," said the wife, "I am king, and you are only my husband, so will you go at once? Go along! for if he was able to make me king he is able to make me emperor; and I will and must be emperor, so go along!"

So he was obliged to go; and as he went he felt very uncomfortable about it, and he thought to himself, "It is not at all the right thing to do; to want to be emperor is really going too far; the flounder will soon be beginning to get tired of this."

With that he came to the sea, and the water was quite black and thick, and the foam flew, and the wind blew, and the man was terrified. But he stood and said,

"O man, O man!—if man you be,
Or flounder, flounder, in the sea—
Such a tiresome wife I've got,
For she wants what I do not."

"What is it now?" said the fish.

"Oh dear!" said the man, "my wife wants to be emperor."

"Go home with you," said the fish, "she is emperor already."

So the man went home, and found the castle adorned with polished marble and alabaster figures, and golden gates. The troops were being marshalled before the door, and they were blowing trumpets and beating drums and cymbals; and when he entered he saw barons and earls and dukes waiting about like servants; and the doors were of bright gold. And he saw his wife sitting upon a throne made of one entire piece of gold, and it was about two miles high; and she had a great golden crown on, which was about three yards high, set with brilliants and carbuncles; and in one hand she held the sceptre, and in the other the globe; and on both sides of her stood pages in two rows, all arranged according to their

size, from the most enormous giant of two
miles high to the tiniest dwarf of the size of
my little finger; and before her stood earls
and dukes in crowds. So the man went up to
her and said, "Well, wife, so now you are
emperor."

"Yes," said she, "now I am emperor."

Then he went and sat down and had a

good look at her, and then he said, "Well now, wife, there is nothing left to be, now you are emperor."

"What are you talking about, husband?" said she; "I am emperor, and next I will be pope! so go and tell the fish so."

"Oh dear!" said the man, "what is it that you don't want? You can never become pope; there is but one pope in Christendom, and the fish can't possibly do it."

"Husband," said she, "no more words about it; I must and will be pope; so go along to the fish."

"Now, wife," said the man, "how can I ask him such a thing? it is too bad—it is asking a little too much; and, besides, he could not do it."

"What rubbish!" said the wife; "if he could make me emperor he can make me pope. Go along and ask him; I am emperor, and you are only my husband, so go you must."

So he went, feeling very frightened, and he shivered and shook, and his knees trembled; and there arose a great wind, and the clouds flew by, and it grew very dark, and the sea rose mountains high, and the ships were tossed about, and the sky was partly blue in the middle, but at the sides very dark and red, as in a great tempest. And he felt very desponding, and stood trembling and said,

"O man, O man—if man you be,
Or flounder, flounder, in the sea—

"Well, what now?" said the fish.

"Oh dear!" said the man, "she wants to be pope."

"Go home with you, she is pope already," said the fish.

So he went home, and he found himself before a great church, with palaces all round. He had to make his way through a crowd of people; and when he got inside he found the place lighted up with thousands and thousands of lights; and his wife was clothed in a golden garment, and sat upon a very high throne, and had three golden crowns on, all in the greatest priestly pomp; and on both sides of her there stood two rows of lights of all sizes—from the size of the longest tower to the smallest rushlight, and all the emperors and kings were kneeling before her and kissing her foot.

"Well, wife," said the man, and sat and stared at her, "so you are pope."

"Yes," said she, "now I am pope!"

And he went on gazing at her till he felt dazzled, as if he were sitting in the sun. And after a little time he said, "Well, now, wife, what is there left to be, now you are pope?"

And she sat up very stiff and straight, and said nothing.

And he said again, "Well, wife, I hope you are contented at last with being pope; you can be nothing more."

"We will see about that," said the wife. With that they both went to bed; but she was as far as ever from being contented, and she could not get to sleep for thinking of what she should like to be next.

The husband, however, slept as fast as a top after his busy day; but the wife tossed and turned from side to side the whole night through, thinking all the while what she could be next, but nothing would occur to her; and when she saw the red dawn she slipped off the bed, and sat before the window to see the sun rise, and as it came up she said, "Ah, I have it! what if I should make the sun and moon to rise—husband!" she cried, and stuck her elbow in his ribs, "wake up, and go to your fish, and tell him I want power over the sun and moon."

The man was so fast asleep that when he started up he fell out of bed. Then he shook himself together, and opened his eyes and said, "Oh,—wife, what did you say?"

"Husband," said she, "if I cannot get the power of making the sun and moon rise when I want them, I shall never have another quiet hour. Go to the fish and tell him so."

"O wife!" said the man, and fell on his knees to her, "the fish can really not do that for you. I grant you he could make you emperor and pope; do be contented with that, I beg of you."

And she became wild with impatience, and screamed out, "I can wait no longer, go at once!"

And so off he went as well as he could for fright. And a dreadful storm arose, so that he could hardly keep his feet; and the houses and trees were blown down, and the mountains trembled, and rocks fell in the sea; the sky was quite black, and it thundered and lightened; and the waves, crowned with foam, ran mountains high. So he cried out, without being able to hear his own words.

"O man, O man!—if man you be,
Or flounder, flounder, in the sea—
Such a tiresome wife I've got,
For she wants what I do not."

"Well, what now?" said the flounder.

"Oh dear!" said the man, "she wants to order about the sun and moon."

"Go home with you!" said the flounder, "you will find her in the old hovel."

And there they are sitting to this very day.

A long time ago, perhaps as much as two thousand years, there was a rich man, and he had a beautiful and pious wife, and they loved each other very much, and they had no children, though they wished greatly for some, and the wife prayed for one day and night. Now, in the courtyard in front of their house stood an almond tree; and one day in winter the wife was standing beneath it, and paring an apple, and as she pared it she cut her finger, and the blood fell upon the snow.

"Ah," said the woman, sighing deeply, and looking down at the blood, "if only I could have a child as red as blood, and as white as snow!"

And as she said these words, her heart suddenly grew light, and she felt sure she should have her wish. So she went back to the house, and when a month had passed the snow was gone; in two months everything was green; in three months the flowers sprang out of the earth; in four months the trees were in full leaf, and the branches were thickly entwined; the little birds began to sing, so that the woods echoed, and the blossoms fell from the trees; when the fifth month had passed the wife stood under the almond tree, and it smelt so sweet that her heart leaped within her, and she fell on her knees for joy; and when the sixth month had gone, the fruit was thick and fine, and she remained still; and the seventh month she gathered the almonds, and ate them eagerly, and was sick and sorrowful; and when the eighth month had passed she called to her husband, and said, weeping, "If I die, bury me under the almond tree."

Then she was comforted and happy until the ninth month had passed, and then she bore a child as white as snow and as red as blood, and when she saw it her joy was so great that she died.

Her husband buried her under the almond tree, and he wept sore; time passed, and he became less sad; and after he had grieved a little more he left off, and then he took another wife.

His second wife bore him a daughter, and his first wife's child was a son, as red as blood and as white as snow. Whenever the wife looked at her daughter she felt great love for her, but whenever she looked at the little boy, evil thoughts came into her heart, of how she could get all her husband's money for her daughter, and how the boy stood in the way; and so she took great hatred to him, and drove him from one corner to another, and gave him a buffet here and a cuff there, so that the poor child was always in disgrace; when he came back after school hours there was no peace for him.

Once, when the wife went into the room upstairs, her little daughter followed her, and said, "Mother, give me an apple."

"Yes, my child," said the mother, and gave her a fine apple out of the chest, and the chest had a great heavy lid with a strong iron lock.

"Mother," said the little girl, "shall not my brother have one too?"

That was what the mother expected, and she said, "Yes, when he comes back from school."

And when she saw from the window that he was coming, an evil thought crossed her mind, and she snatched the apple, and took it from her little daughter, saying, "You shall not have it before your brother."

Then she threw the apple into the chest, and shut the lid. Then the little boy came in at the door, and she said to him in a kind tone, but with evil looks, "My son, will you have an apple?"

"Mother," said the boy, "how terrible you look! yes, give me an apple!"

Then she spoke as kindly as before, holding up the cover of the chest, "Come here and take out one for yourself."

And as the boy was stooping over the open chest, crash went the lid down, so that his head flew off among the red apples. But then the woman felt great terror, and wondered how she could escape the blame. And she went to the chest of drawers in her bedroom and took a white handkerchief out of the nearest drawer, and fitting the head to the neck, she bound them with the handkerchief, so that nothing should be seen, and set him on a chair before the door with the apple in his hand.

Then came little Marjory into the kitchen to her mother, was was standing before the fire stirring a pot of hot water.

"Mother," said Marjory, "my brother is sitting before the door and he has an apple in his hand, and looks very pale; I asked him to give me the apple, but he did not answer me; it seems very strange."

"Go again to him," said the mother, "and if he will not answer you, give him a box on the ear."

So Marjory went again and said,

"Brother, give me the apple."

But as he took no notice, she gave him a box on the ear, and his head fell off, at which she was greatly terrified, and began to cry and scream, and ran to her mother, and said, "O mother! I have knocked my brother's head off!" and cried and screamed, and would not cease.

"O Marjory!" said her mother, "what have you done? but keep quiet, that no one may see there is anything the matter; it can't be helped now; we will put him out of the way safely."

When the father came home and sat down to table, he said, "Where is my son?"

But the mother was filling a great dish full of black broth, and Marjory was crying bitterly, for she could not refrain. Then the father said again, "Where is my son?"

"Oh," said the mother, "he is gone into the country to his great-uncle's to stay for a little while."

"What should he go for?" said the father, "and without bidding me good-bye, too!"

"Oh, he wanted to go so much, and he asked me to let him stay there six weeks; he will be well taken care of."

"Dear me," said the father, "I am quite sad about it; it was not right of him to go without bidding me good-bye."

With that he began to eat, saying, "Marjory, what are you crying for? Your brother will come back some time."

After a while he said, "Well, wife, the food is very good; give me some more."

And the more he ate the more he wanted, until he had eaten it all up, and he threw the bones under the table. Then Marjory went to her chest of drawers, and took one of her best handkerchiefs from the bottom drawer, and picked up all the bones from under the table and tied them up in her handkerchief, and went out at the door crying bitterly. She laid them in the green grass under the al-

mond tree, and immediately her heart grew
light again, and she wept no more. Then the
almond tree began to wave to and fro, and
the boughs drew together and then parted,
just like a clapping of hands for joy; then a
cloud rose from the tree, and in the midst of
the cloud there burned a fire, and out of the
fire a beautiful bird arose, and, singing most
sweetly, soared high into the air; and when
he had flown away, the almond tree remained as it was before, but the handkerchief full of bones was gone. Marjory felt
quite glad and light-hearted, just as if her
brother were still alive. So she went back
merrily into the house and had her dinner.

The bird, when it flew away, perched on the roof of a goldsmith's house, and began to sing,

> *"It was my mother who murdered me;*
> *It was my father who ate of me;*
> *It was my sister Marjory*
> *Who all my bones in pieces found;*
> *Them in a handkerchief she bound,*
> *And laid them under the almond tree.*
> *Kywitt, kywitt, kywitt, I cry,*
> *Oh what a beautiful bird am I!"*

The goldsmith was sitting in his shop making a golden chain, and when he heard the bird, who was sitting on his roof and singing, he started up to go and look, and as he passed over his threshold he lost one of his slippers; and he went into the middle of the street with a slipper on one foot and only a sock on the other; with his apron on, and the gold chain in one hand and the pincers in the other; and so he stood in the sunshine looking up at the bird.

"Bird," said he, "how beautifully you sing; do sing that piece over again."

"No," said the bird, "I do not sing for nothing twice; if you will give me that gold chain I will sing again."

"Very well," said the goldsmith, "here is the gold chain; now do as you said."

Down came the bird and took the gold chain in his right claw, perched in front of the goldsmith, and sang,

> *"It was my mother who murdered me;*
> *It was my father who ate of me;*

It was my sister Marjory
Who all my bones in pieces found;
Them in a handkerchief she bound,
And laid them under the almond tree.
Kywitt, kywitt, kywitt, I cry,
Oh what a beautiful bird am I!"

Then the bird flew to a shoemaker's, and perched on his roof, and sang,

"It was my mother who murdered me;
It was my father who ate of me;
It was my sister Marjory
Who all my bones in pieces found;
Them in a handkerchief she bound,
And laid them under the almond tree.
Kywitt, kywitt, kywitt, I cry,
Oh what a beautiful bird am I!"

When the shoemaker heard, he ran out of his door in his shirt sleeves and looked up at the roof of his house, holding his hand to shade his eyes from the sun.

"Bird," said he, "how beautifully you sing!"

Then he called in at his door, "Wife, come out directly; here is a bird singing beautifully; only listen."

Then he called his daughter, all his children, and acquaintance, both young men and maidens, and they came up the street and gazed on the bird, and saw how beautiful it was with red and green feathers, and round its throat was as it were gold, and its eyes twinkled in its head like stars.

"Bird," said the shoemaker, "do sing that piece over again."

"No," said the bird, "I may not sing for

nothing twice; you must give me some-thing."

"Wife," said the man, "go into the shop; on the top shelf stands a pair of red shoes; bring them here."

So the wife went and brought the shoes.

"Now bird," said the man, "sing us that piece again."

And the bird came down and took the shoes in his left claw, and flew up again to the roof, and sang,

> *"It was my mother who murdered me;*
> *It was my father who ate of me;*
> *It was my sister Marjory*
> *Who all my bones in pieces found;*
> *Them in a handkerchief she bound,*
> *And laid them under the almond tree.*
> *Kywitt, kywitt, kywitt, I cry,*
> *Oh what a beautiful bird am I!"*

And when he had finished he flew away, with the chain in his right claw and the shoes in his left claw, and he flew till he reached a mill, and the mill went "clip-clap, clip-clap, clip-clap." And in the mill sat twenty millers-men hewing a millstone—"hick-hack, hick-hack, hick-hack," while the mill was going "clip-clap, clip-clap, clip-clap." And the bird perched on a linden tree that stood in front of the mill, and sang,

> *"It was my mother who murdered me;"*

Here one of the men looked up.

> *"It was my father who ate of me;"*

Then two more looked up and listened.

> *"It was my sister Marjory"*

Here four more looked up.

> *"Who all my bones in pieces found;*
> *Them in a handkerchief she bound,"*

Now there were only eight left hewing.

> *"And laid them under the almond tree."*

Now only five.

> *"Kywitt, kywitt, kywitt, I cry,"*

Now only one.

> *"Oh what a beautiful bird am I!"*

At length the last one left off, and he only heard the end.

"Bird," said he, "how beautifully you sing; let me hear it all; sing that again!"

"No," said the bird, "I may not sing it twice for nothing; if you will give me the millstone I will sing it again."

"Indeed," said the man, "if it belonged to me alone you should have it."

"All right," said the others, "if he sings again he shall have it."

Then the bird came down, and all the twenty millers heaved up the stone with poles—"yo! heave-ho! yo! heave-ho!" and the bird stuck his head through the hole in the middle, and with the millstone round his neck he flew up to the tree and sang,

> *"It was my mother who murdered me;*
> *It was my father who ate of me;*
> *It was my sister Marjory*
> *Who all my bones in pieces found;*
> *Them in a handkerchief she bound,*
> *And laid them under the almond tree.*
> *Kywitt, kywitt, kywitt, I cry,*
> *Oh what a beautiful bird am I!"*

And when he had finished, he spread his wings, having in the right claw the chain, and in the left claw the shoes, and round his neck the millstone, and he flew away to his father's house.

In the parlor sat the father, the mother, and Marjory at the table; the father said, "How light-hearted and cheerful I feel."

"Nay," said the mother, "I feel very low, just as if a great storm were coming."

But Marjory sat weeping; and the bird came flying, and perched on the roof.

"Oh," said the father, "I feel so joyful, and the sun is shining so bright; it is as if I were going to meet with an old friend."

"Nay," said the wife, "I am terrified, my teeth chatter, and there is fire in my veins," and she tore open her dress to get air; and Marjory sat in a corner and wept, with her plate before her, until it was quite full of tears. Then the bird perched on the almond tree, and sang,

"It was my mother who murdered me;"

And the mother stopped her ears and hid her eyes, and would neither see nor hear; nevertheless, the noise of a fearful storm was in her ears, and in her eyes a quivering and burning as of lightning.

"It was my father who ate of me;"

"O mother!" said the father, "there is a beautiful bird singing so finely, and the sun shines, and everything smells as sweet as cinnamon.

Marjory hid her face in her lap and wept, and the father said, "I must go out to see the bird."

"Oh do not go!" said the wife, "I feel as if the house were on fire."

But the man went out and looked at the bird.

"Who all my bones in pieces found;
Them in a handkerchief she bound,
And laid them under the almond tree.
Kywitt, kywitt, kywitt, I cry,
Oh what a beautiful bird am I!"

With that the bird let fall the gold chain upon his father's neck, and it fitted him exactly. So he went indoors and said, "Look what a beautiful chain the bird has given me."

Then his wife was so terrified that she fell all along on the floor, and her cap came off. Then the bird began again to sing,

"It was my mother who murdered me;"

"Oh," groaned the mother, "that I were a thousand fathoms under ground, so as not to be obliged to hear it."

"It was my father who ate of me;"

Then the woman lay as if she were dead.

"It was my sister Marjory"

"Oh," said Marjory, "I will go out, too, and see if the bird will give me anything." And so she went.

"Who all my bones in pieces found;
Them in a handkerchief she bound,"

Then he threw the shoes down to her.

"And laid them under the almond tree,
Kywitt, kywitt, kywitt, I cry,
Oh what a beautiful bird am I!"

And poor Marjory all at once felt happy and joyful, and put on her red shoes, and danced and jumped for joy.

"Oh dear," said she, "I felt so sad before I went outside, and now my heart is so light! He is a charming bird to have given me a pair of red shoes."

But the mother's hair stood on end, and looked like flame, and she said, "Even if the world is coming to an end, I must go out for a little relief."

Just as she came outside the door, crash went the millstone on her head, and crushed her flat. The father and daughter rushed out, and saw smoke and flames of fire rise up; but when that had gone by, there stood the little brother; and he took his father and Marjory by the hand, and they felt very happy and content, and went indoors, and sat to the table, and had their dinner.

here was once a peasant who owned a faithful dog called Sultan, now grown so old that he had lost all his teeth, and could lay hold of nothing. One day the man was standing at the door of his house with his wife, and he said, "I shall kill old Sultan to-morrow; he is of no good any longer."

His wife felt sorry for the poor dog, and answered, "He has served us for so many years, and has kept with us so faithfully, he deserves food and shelter in his old age."

"Dear me, you do not seem to understand the matter," said the husband; "he has never a tooth, and no thief would mind him in the least, so I do not see why he should not be made away with. If he has served us well, we have given him plenty of good food."

The poor dog, who was lying stretched out in the sun not far off, heard all they said, and was very sad to think that the next day would be his last. He bethought him of his great friend the wolf, and slipped out in the evening to the wood to see him, and related to him the fate that was awaiting him.

"Listen to me, old fellow," said the wolf;

"be of good courage, I will help you in your need. I have thought of a way. Early to-morrow morning your master is going hay-making with his wife, and they will take their child with them, so that no one will be left at home. They will be sure to lay the child in the shade behind the hedge while they are at work; you must lie by its side, just as if you were watching it. Then I will come out of the wood and steal away the child; you must rush after me, as if to save it from me. Then I must let it fall, and you must bring it back again to its parents, who will think that you have saved it, and will be much too grateful to do you any harm; on the contrary, you will be received into full favor, and they will never let you want for anything again."

The dog was pleased with the plan, which was carried out accordingly. When the father saw the wolf running away with his child he cried out, and when old Sultan brought it back again, he was much pleased with him, and patted him, saying, "Not a hair of him shall be touched; he shall have food and shelter as long as he lives." And he said to his wife, "Go home directly and make some good stew for old Sultan, something that does not need biting; and get the pillow from my bed for him to lie on."

From that time old Sultan was made so comfortable that he had nothing left to wish for. Before long the wolf paid him a visit, to congratulate him that all had gone so well.

"But, old fellow," said he, "you must wink at my making off by chance with a fat sheep of your master's; perhaps one will escape some fine day."

"Don't reckon on that," answered the dog; "I cannot consent to it; I must remain true to my master."

But the wolf, not supposing it was said in earnest, came sneaking in the night to carry off the sheep. But the master, who had been warned by the faithful Sultan of the wolf's intention, was waiting for him, and gave him a fine hiding with the threshing-flail. So the wolf had to make his escape, calling out to the dog, "You shall pay for this, you traitor!"

The next morning the wolf sent the wild boar to call out the dog; and to appoint a meeting in the wood to receive satisfaction from him. Old Sultan could find no second but a cat with three legs; and as they set off together, the poor thing went limping along, holding her tail up in the air. The wolf and his second were already on the spot; when they saw their antagonists coming, and caught sight of the elevated tail of the cat, they thought it was a sabre they were bringing with them. And as the poor thing came limping on three legs, they supposed it was lifting a big stone to throw at them. This frightened them very much; the wild boar crept among the leaves, and the wolf clambered up into a tree. And when the dog and cat came up, they were surprised not to see any one there. However, the wild boar was not perfectly hidden in the leaves, and the tips of his ears peeped out. And when the cat caught sight of one, she thought it was a mouse, and sprang upon it, seizing it with her teeth. Out leaped the wild boar with a dreadful cry, and ran away shouting, "There is the culprit in the tree!"

And the dog and the cat looking up caught sight of the wolf, who came down, quite ashamed of his timidity, and made peace with the dog once more.